Rainbow Nightmares

Xine Fury

Rainbow Nightmares
Copyright © 2024 by Xine Fury

ISBN: 978-1-967029-06-8

Rainbow Nightmares

Contents

Escapism

"What eludes the hawk is found by the bat."

"What the heck does that mean?" Brie asked.

Wickett shrugged. "That's all it says." He turned the paper over to make sure nothing was written on the back.

"Well, bats hunt in the dark," Kara offered. "And hawks are known for their eyesight."

"Oh!" Quin said. "Find the light switch."

"On it," Wickett said, flipping off the light.

With the lights off, they were suddenly able to see the number "388426" written on the wall in glowing green letters.

"Cool, glow-in-the-dark paint," Brie said.

They turned the light back on and typed the number into the keypad next to the exit door. Instead of the door opening, however, a bookcase slid aside, revealing another hidden door.

"I've always wanted one of those in my house," Quin said.

Brie opened the new door and looked inside. Then she turned back to her three companions, looking confused. "It's just a restroom," she told them.

"Thank god, I'm about to burst," Kara said, and went inside.

"I was sure that would be the exit," Wickett said.

"We're certainly getting our money's worth," Quin said. "How long have we been in here, anyway?"

Brie looked around the room, hoping to spot a clock. The staff had taken their phones at the front desk to discourage cheating, and none of them wore watches. The escape room was extremely cluttered, with a dozen bookshelves, three desks, a couch, four chairs, several end tables, and a water fountain. There were books everywhere, on the shelves, on the tables, even stacked on the floor. There were four paintings on the walls, some of which had clues hidden behind them, but the paintings themselves also had clues hidden in the art.

"Two hours, at least," Wickett said. "My stomach's starting to growl."

So far they'd solved fourteen riddles. Most had just led to other clues. One had opened the panel covering the exit door, but the door itself was still locked.

Kara emerged from the restroom. "Guys, there's another clue in there," she said. The other three pushed past her and looked around. The restroom had four stalls and two sinks. The fourth stall didn't hold a toilet, but led to another door. This door was also locked.

Each stall had a riddle written on the wall, in the style of graffiti. The bathroom ceiling had the number 15,181 written on it, and the number 47 was painted on the floor.

"Maybe it's a math problem," Quin suggested. "Like, we divide the top number by the bottom number."

"Great, my best subject," Brie said, her voice tinged with sarcasm.

"Give me a minute," Kara said. They didn't have any pens, so she traced some numbers in the air as she thought. "Three hundred and twenty-three," she said finally.

"And what do we do with that?" Wickett asked.

They looked around for more clues. Brie walked back out to the main room and typed the number into the keypad, but nothing happened.

"Let's look at those riddles again," Wickett said. He, Kara, and Quin each took a stall. "Mine says, 'What has four legs in the morning…'" Wickett began.

"Everybody knows that one," Kara called out from the next stall. "The answer is a man."

"I'm the only man in our group," Wickett said. "Does that mean I'm supposed to do something?"

"I don't know," Kara said. "My riddle is, 'Birds of a feather, flock together, but Suzy could not fly. Her flock all wore sweaters, when they got together, and Suzy asked what am I?'"

"A penguin?" Wickett suggested.

"No a sheep," Quin said. "Here's mine. 'You went to church every Sunday but then voted red. You looked down on the needy while you were well-fed. You called yourself Christian, and now you are dead. You thought you'd be there, but you're here instead.'"

"Hell?" Kara guessed.

"Man Sheep Hell?" Brie asked, as her friends emerged from the stalls.

"Not sheep, Ewe!" Quin said. "Man-ewe-hell. Manual!"

"Manual for what?" Wickett asked. "Did anyone come across any manuals in the other room?"

"Maybe it means we have to solve the problem by hand," Quin said.

"Or a car reference?" Brie offered. "You know, manual, not automatic."

"Let's look through the books again," Kara said. "Look for instruction manuals and anything about cars."

They spread out across the escape room, looking at the titles of books. After a few minutes, Brie piped up. "This has to be it," she said. "It's a toilet repair manual."

She flipped through the book. It was over two hundred pages, but most of them were blank. In the middle of the book, there was a single page of text. It read, "You don't need a repair manual, because these toilets are guaranteed never to break. Flush them as many times as you want. In fact, go flush them a few times right now, just because."

"That's a weird thing to put in a book," Wickett said.

"Should we try flushing them?" Quin asked.

"I have a thought," Kara said. "The math problem. The answer was three two three. We'll flush the first one three times, the second one twice, then the third one three times."

"Worth a try," Quin said.

The women took the first three stalls, while Wickett stood by the locked door in the fourth stall. When they were done flushing, the door clicked, and Wickett was able to push it open.

The door opened to a dining room, with a long table surrounded by eight chairs. Four of the seats had place settings. The center of the table held a bowl of fruit and a plate full of cheeseburgers. A placard on the table read, "Help Yourself."

"This just goes on and on," Kara said, looking around.

"Hard to believe the whole thing fits in the mall," Quin added. "Wasn't there a shoe store next door? Seems like this room would overlap with it."

"I don't know, I'm all turned around," Wickett said.

"Are we actually allowed to eat the food?" Brie asked.

"For forty dollars a ticket, I imagine so," Kara said.

"Well, I am pretty hungry," Wickett said, pulling out a chair.

"You see any actual puzzles in here?" Brie asked, looking around. There was a smaller table against one wall, on which sat a bowl of ice and four pitchers – one full of water, one cola, one lemonade, and one punch. Some cabinets on the walls held more dishes and silverware. There was another door on the wall to the right, one that should have led back to the study, but there hadn't been a door in the study that it could have led to. Wickett was right, it was easy to get turned around in here.

The other three looked under their glasses and the serving bowls, but they couldn't find any clues either. "Maybe it's a freebie," Wickett said, taking a bite out of a burger. "For solving the restroom puzzle, we earned a free lunch."

"What about this door?" Brie asked, twisting the knob. Of course it was locked. There was a shelf attached to the door, on which sat four shot glasses, each nesting in holes cut in the wood.

"There were still a couple of riddles we never solved back in the study," Kara said. "Were any of them food-related?"

"Not that I remember," Quin said, eyeing the drinks. "But wasn't there a color one?"

"Yeah," Kara said. "Something like how the yellow sun turns red as it sets on the clear lake surrounded by the brown dirt."

"Is that the order?" Brie asked.

"Go check if you want," Kara said. "But I think so."

"Sounds right to me," Wickett added.

Brie walked over to the pitchers and grabbed two of them. Seeing what she was up to, Quin put down her burger and helped her with the other two. Kara also stood and followed them to the door. Only Wickett kept eating.

They poured a bit of lemonade into the first shot glass, followed by punch in the next, then the water, and finally the cola. As soon as they finished pouring the cola, the door unlocked.

"Yes!" Brie shouted, then turned and kissed Kara on the lips. Then Kara turned to kiss Quin, and Quin kissed Brie. That last kiss lingered for a while.

"Okay, okay," Kara said. "My turn again." She leaned in to kiss Brie.

"Tone it down," Wickett said. "As the only one here not in your little polycule, I'm morally obligated to act as chaperone. You don't want to get us kicked out of here."

"Would that be so bad at this point?" Brie asked, setting her pitchers down on the table.

"Are you not having any fun?" Kara asked, putting her hand on Brie's shoulder.

"It's fun," Brie said. "But it's dragging on a little long."

"I agree," Quin said. "I wish we knew how much longer this thing is."

"Yeah, I promised Rick I'd be home by seven," Wickett said. "We have a special dinner planned."

"Anniversary?" Kara asked.

"Celebration," Wickett replied. "He got a bonus at work."

"Nice," Quin said. "Well, if the next room isn't the exit, we can use that 'chicken out' code they gave us." The keypad in the study had a combination they could press if they wanted to leave early, but doing so would cost them. Those who completed the entire escape room received a commemorative badge, and their names were put on the wall in the lobby.

"Shall we see?" Kara asked.

"Can we finish eating first?" Wickett asked. "For all we know, the next room could take another hour."

"Actually, I wouldn't mind that," Kara said. The women sat back down and everyone finished their meals, chatting about the puzzles they'd solved so far. When they were done, they stood and opened the door.

The next room was a bedroom. There were two bunk beds on opposite walls. There was another door on the far wall, and a computer desk sat in one corner. The computer's screensaver was a scrolling message that read, "Rest if you're weary."

"I don't get it," Brie said.

"Maybe if we each get in a bed, it unlocks the door," Kara suggested.

"Does that computer work?" Wickett asked, tapping a key. A password prompt came up. He sat down and started trying passwords, using answers to the riddles they'd solved so far. Brie and Kara called out suggestions.

"Maybe the computer unlocks if we lie down on the

beds," Brie offered.

"Aaaaand we've just turned the corner onto Tedious Lane," Quin said, sitting on a bed.

Wickett had tried fifteen passwords so far, but no luck. Fortunately, there didn't seem to be a limit to how many attempts he could make.

"That's weird," Kara said. "Did you notice the date?" She pointed to the lower right-hand side of the monitor.

"Somebody must have set the clock wrong," Wickett said. The date displayed was one week in the future, and the time was nine PM.

"Okay, well, let's just try the bed thing," Brie said. "If it doesn't work, we'll go back to the study and use the 'chicken out' code."

"Deal," Quin said. Each of them climbed onto a bed.

"I hope they wash these after each group," Kara said, sniffing the sheets.

Once all four were in place, the lights turned off. They listened for the click of the unlocking door, but didn't hear anything. However, with the lights off, they saw something that hadn't seen before. A faint yellow light flickered from underneath one of the beds.

"I'll check it out," Brie said, climbing off her mattress. The lights immediately came back on. Brie crawled under the bed and saw a small round light on the wall, flashing rhythmically. "It looks like a pattern," she told her friends. "Anybody know Morse code?"

"Okay, that's it, I'm done," Quin said. "Back to the study, we've got better things to do with our lives."

They all agreed that they'd had enough fun for their money. Back in the study, there was a little sticker above the keypad that read, "To end your adventure early, type 1111."

Kara typed in the code. The digital readout asked, "Are you sure? 1=Yes 2=No."

She hit 1, only for the readout to display, "Too bad. Find your own way out."

"They're joking right?" Quin asked, pushing on the door.

"There has to at least be an emergency exit somewhere," Kara said, looking around. "Isn't that the law?"

"I found a book on Morse code," Brie said, pulling a volume off one of the shelves.

"I don't care," Quin said. She started waving her arms, looking around for a security camera. "Can you see us? We want out! Unlock that door right now!"

"Maybe they went home," Kara said.

"I'm going leave them such a bad review on their website," Wickett said.

"Oh, aren't you a badass," Quin replied. "I'm going to sue them until this entire business is a smoking hole in the ground."

"Maybe we can force the door open," Kara suggested. "Anything crowbar-like in here?"

"They'll sue us if we cause any damage," Wickett said.

"They can try," Quin said. "I'm pre-law, I know my rights."

"If you cause enough damage, they might come in here and stop us," Kara said. "We might get arrested, but at least we'd be out of here."

"You hear that?" Quin said, shouting at the ceiling. "Let us out or we'll tear up the place!" To emphasize her point, she grabbed a book off the desk and started ripping out the pages.

"Are we really to that point already?" Wickett asked.

"I passed it half an hour ago," Quin said. Unfortunately, there weren't a lot of breakables in the study, and ripping up books was only cathartic for so long. Running out of steam, Quin sat on the couch and sulked. Kara sat down next to her and put her arm around her shoulder.

"They're probably just at lunch or something," Kara said. "They'll come back, they'll see what you did, we'll pay a fine and go home."

"I'd like to see them try to fine me," Quin said. She stood

up. "I'm going to go break some dishes."

"Hold on," Kara said. "Where's Brie?"

They found her in the bedroom, her legs sticking out from under the bed.

"You okay down there, Brie?" Kara asked, getting down on one knee.

"Yeah," Brie replied. "Try typing this in the computer. 'There is no escape.'"

Kara sat down at the computer and typed it in. Her first attempt failed, but then she tried it with no spaces, and it worked. The screensaver went away, and they saw what looked like a bulletin board filled with newspaper headlines. As they clicked each headline, the article expanded and filled the screen.

Quin gasped. The first headline was, "Four College Students Disappear At Local Mall." The accompanying photo showed Quin along with Kara, Brie, and Wickett. The article was dated a week in the future.

"These people have a sick sense of humor," Wickett said.

They flipped through more articles, and all of them were on the same subject. Some centered on their families and their reactions to the news, others on the ongoing police investigations.

"I didn't pay for this," Quin said, picking up the monitor. She looked like she would throw it onto the floor before Wickett stopped her.

"We might need it for more clues," he said.

"Fuck your clues!" Quin shouted. "I'm done with this!"

"Hey guys," Brie said, now standing in the doorway. "Did you notice somebody cleared away the food?"

The other three joined her in the dining room. The food was gone and the table was clean. "When did they do that?" Kara asked.

Wickett scratched his head. "Was it like that when we came through just now, or did they do it while we were looking at the computer?"

"I don't remember," Brie said.

Kara cocked her head. "I mean, it had to be while we were in the study, right?"

"Either way we should have heard them," Wickett said.

Quin banged on the wall, shouting into the dining room. "Where are you? Get back in here!"

No answer came.

Hours passed, though they couldn't say how many. The computer's clock ran fast, jumping ahead hours or even days at a time. They solved a few more puzzles, opening the door into a kitchen. A few hours more, and they opened another door, this one leading to a living room. The more rooms they opened, the less sense the layout made. Not only should the bedroom have overlapped the study, but the living room should have occupied the same space as the bedroom.

Every few hours, the dining room became restocked with food. After the burgers came pizza, and after that came hot dogs. The food only appeared when the four were in other rooms.

"I say we keep one of us in the dining room at all times," Quin said, taking the last bite of her hot dog. "Catch 'em in the act. Find whatever hidden door they're popping out of." They'd already felt along every wall and opened every cabinet, looking for hidden panels.

"Don't you get it?" Brie asked in exasperation. "This is not natural. None of this is natural. The rooms can't be where they are. None of this can happen!"

"What are you saying?" Wickett asked, standing up from the table.

"We're not going to catch them," Brie said. "Because we're dealing with something supernatural. Ghosts, aliens, I don't know, maybe we're in Hell. But we're not going to win. We're never going to win. We're at the mercy of... whoever." Her rant ran out of steam on the last word, and she stood with her back against the wall, staring at the floor.

"Fine," Quin said, pushing her empty plate away. "You can give up if you want to. But I'm not ready to throw in the towel. If I'm going to lose, it won't be because I stopped trying."

"The overlapping rooms thing could just be an optical illusion," Kara offered. "Two rooms look parallel, but they're actually angled so that there's a triangle of empty space between them. Or maybe one even goes under the other." She demonstrated with her hands as she talked.

"I don't know," Wickett said. "If it's a trick, it's pretty convincing."

Kara waved him off. "I've seen stage magicians do some amazing things. I'm not going to call this supernatural until I see something really amazing."

Just then the lights flickered and went out. It was pitch black, and the only sound was their breathing. After about ten seconds, the lights came back on. The food was gone, and the dirty dishes had been taken away.

Kara and Quin stared at each other, each trying to think of a rational explanation. Brie burst into tears. Kara got out of her chair and pulled Brie into a hug, while Quin just sat in silence, fuming. Wickett sat back down and put his face in his hands.

"Even if it *is* ghosts," Quin said quietly, "that doesn't mean they get to win."

They slept, they ate, they solved puzzles, they ate again, they solved more puzzles, they slept. Time had lost all meaning. Opening new rooms just meant more disappointment.

"There's worse prisons we could be in," Wickett said, strumming on a harp. They were in a music room, complete with a grand piano and a pipe organ.

"I wouldn't mind unlocking a laundry room soon," Kara said, sniffing her shirt. "Or a shower."

Brie sat at the piano, thumbing through one of the books of sheet music. Over the last few hours, she'd already played every piece of music in the room, on both the piano and the organ. Her fingers were getting tired, but she was the only one in the group who could play.

But for the first time in what seemed like weeks, the group was having fun. It wasn't exactly a party, but more of a tired levity, the kind of camaraderie that only the doomed understand. They sang along to some of the piano music, even making up lyrics to classical pieces. Brie's hands were numb, but she wanted to keep the vibe going, so she started playing pop songs.

First she played a breakup song with catchy lyrics. Everyone tried to out-sing each other, getting louder and louder as it went on. Then she played a classic party anthem that brought up everyone's spirits. Finally she played a popular 1970s song about tropical drinks, personal ads, and cheating lovers. Everyone knew the lyrics and belted them out with gusto.

On the last word of the song, the piano made a hitching sound, followed by two clicks and a thump. A panel above the keys popped open.

"*That* solved a puzzle?" Wickett asked.

"You can't even have fun in this place without puzzles getting in the way," Quin griped.

"How were we supposed to figure that out for ourselves?" Brie asked.

"Well, there's a painting of a pineapple on the wall," Wickett said. "And a coconut on the cover of the sheet music. Then there's…"

"No one cares," Quin said, focusing on the now-open panel. Behind the panel was a card, on which was printed a numerical code:

51931165

Kara rolled her eyes. "Back to the study, I guess." The group walked the winding path through the myriad of unlocked rooms until they finally reached the study. Wickett held his breath as he typed in the code.

Beep. Click. Thunk. The word "Congratulations" briefly showed on the LCD display. Everyone jumped as the door receded into the wall, giving them a clear view into the lobby.

"I don't believe it," Kara said. They stepped into the lobby.

There were no employees behind the front counter, and no customers were in the lobby. The primary lights were off, with only the security lights illuminating the lobby. Outside the escape room, the mall itself was in a similar state. No people, dim lighting. The silence was eerie.

"So it's after hours," Wickett said. "But surely there's a security guard or something."

"Why are all the stores still open?" Brie asked. All up and down the mall, none of the gates were down.

"I don't think they are," Kara replied. "There's no employees, and they're not well lit… It's like they just forgot to lower their gates."

"Let's just get out of here," Quin said. They walked through the empty mall until they reached one of the side entrances. Except the entrance was no longer there. Where there had once been a glass wall with three doors, now stood a blank brick wall.

"No," Brie said. Then she ran over to the wall and banged on it with her fists. "No! No no no!"

Kara walked over and pulled her away from the wall. Holding her in a tight hug, she said, "It's okay, it's okay, we'll be okay. We'll figure this out."

"No we won't," Quin said, causing Kara to look at her strangely. "We've been 'figuring it out' for, what, days? Weeks? I don't even know. We're going to find a way out of this mall, and then the whole city is going to be an escape room. Fuck that, I'm done."

"So… what," Wickett asked. "What do you mean, done?

This isn't like quitting a job or walking out of a bad movie. We're stuck here until we find a way to leave."

"Then we're stuck here," Quin said. "I can think of worse places to live. They feed us, there's bathrooms, probably even showers in here somewhere. Maybe there's no laundry but new clothes are free."

"Fine, you give up," Wickett said. "I don't have that option. I have to see Rick again. You at least have each other. I'm going to check the other exits before I wimp out."

"Wimp out?" Quin asked, her voice rising. But Wickett was already walking away.

Brie was starting to hyperventilate, and Kara sat down on the floor with her, their backs against the wall.

"I just want to see my family again," Brie sobbed.

"I know, I know," Kara said, holding her tight. "Me too."

They sat in silence for about ten minutes, then heard footsteps echoing down the hall. "Guys," Wickett shouted. "You're going to want to see this."

The mall's other exits were similarly walled off, except for one. The largest exit, which was adjacent to the food court, had been replaced with a metal door identical to the one in the escape room. Once again, there was a keypad next to the door.

Wickett held up a folded piece of paper. "This was taped to the door," he said. He unfolded it and read it aloud to his friends.

Dear customers,

This is the final door. Beyond it lies your freedom. To learn the code, simply solve fifty-four more puzzles, one for every store in the mall.

Thank you for your patronage.

- The management at Endless Fun Escape Rooms

"To be fair," Wickett said, "compared to what we've done

already, fifty-four puzzles isn't too bad."

Quin slapped him.

Of course, there are puzzles and then there are *puzzles*. Each shop in the mall had its own puzzles and sub-puzzles, nested within each other. Completing each shop took anywhere from a week to a month, though they never knew for sure since there was no way to gauge the passage of time.

Every once in a while, fresh food would appear on a table in the food court. They found showers and even a laundry machine in one of the employee break areas. They slept on comfortable display beds in a furniture store.

After what seemed like years, they found all the parts of the fifty-four-digit code that unlocked the door. It whooshed open, and they found themselves staring into the lobby of the escape room.

As they walked through the door, Brie glanced behind her. The door was already sliding shut, but she was sure she saw the study again, rather than the food court. Then she looked down at her clothing. She'd been wearing an outfit she'd taken off the racks of a designer boutique, but she now wore the jeans and T-shirt she'd originally worn to the escape room.

The lobby was well-lit, and the employee smiled at them from behind the counter. On the wall behind her, a clock showed the date and time. They'd been in the escape room for a little over an hour.

"You made it!" their host said with a plastic smile. "Did you have a good time?"

For a minute the quartet just stared at her. Then Quin spoke up. "It was... an experience."

The next day, the following reviews were posted to the Endless Fun Escape Room's website:

"A great value for the money. Absolute heaven for puzzle

lovers. Life changing. ****" - Kara C.

"I almost gave up. Glad I saw it through. I'd like to meet the owners sometime. ****" - Quin L.

"So many doors. I can now hear colors. The square root of Albuquerque is ham. Why don't more cantaloupes go to private school? *****" - Brie M.

"A once-in-a-lifetime experience. You'll never want to visit another escape room again. ****" - T. Wickett

Survivors

SeaDreams billed itself as the deepest underwater hotel in the world. Mariah didn't know if that was true, but she was certainly impressed by her accommodations. The pod was bigger than her apartment, with three large rooms and a full bath. The living room featured three curved windows, with a comfortable couch for watching sea life. She was so far down that barely any light trickled down from the surface, but the hotel had external lights she could turn on for a better look.

I wish Deanna could have seen this, Mariah thought. She wasn't sure if she meant it, though. Their breakup was still an open wound, and Mariah wished she'd had more time to process it before the trip. She'd have canceled the reservation if she could have, but the booking was non-refundable, and it had been very expensive. After several days of indecision, she'd decided it was better to go alone than to waste it. Besides, she hoped a solo adventure would take her mind off things. So far it hadn't worked.

At six PM, a pair of divers entered through the airlock and brought Mariah dinner. The divers – who also owned the business – stayed with her for about an hour, pointing out some of the passing fish. Mariah was glad to have someone to talk to and was disappointed when they finally left.

Now alone, Mariah changed into her pajamas and made

herself comfortable on the couch. She watched the fish for a while, but it didn't take her mind off her ex-girlfriend. Then she tried reading a book on her tablet, but she found herself rereading the same passages several times without anything sinking in. The room didn't have wi-fi, but it did include a DVD player and a selection of nautical-themed movies. She picked one at random and watched it without really watching it.

I can't do this, she thought. She'd come on this vacation so she wouldn't waste it, and she still felt like she was wasting it. No more. She turned off the movie, opened up her laptop, and started writing a lengthy e-mail to Deanna. She wasn't sure if she'd ever send it, but just typing it out would give her closure. She wrote all the things she'd wished she'd brought up during their final few arguments, getting all the "should've saids" out of her system. Then her rant took a friendly turn. She wished Deanna a wonderful life and went on to describe her vacation so far.

The letter gradually morphed into a travelogue. Mariah described every minute of her trip so far. The flight, the tourist attractions she'd visited after landing, the sights she'd seen while scuba diving around the SeaDreams hotel, and finally the hotel itself. A small part of her wanted to rub Deanna's nose in the fact that she was missing such a wonderful trip. But for the most part, writing was making Mariah feel better, and she didn't want to stop just yet.

But eventually she ran out of words. She ended the letter on a high note, once again wishing Deanna well. Then she closed her laptop and watched the fish swim by. Going forward, she knew she was going to enjoy the vacation, bittersweet though it was. She fell asleep watching the fish, woke up around midnight, and went back to sleep in the bedroom.

She woke up again around six AM. Something seemed off about the place. She heard a motor running that she hadn't heard the night before. She went to the pantry, where a digital control panel informed her that the hotel was running on the backup generator. There was a phone on the wall that could only be used to call her hosts, but when she picked it up, it didn't seem to be working.

It was weird, but she wasn't too concerned. According to the schedule, her hosts would show up at around seven to bring her breakfast, then they'd take her on another underwater excursion around the nearby reefs. Mariah changed clothes and packed up her backpack, then stuffed it into a waterproof bag. She wouldn't be returning to the hotel after the excursion, as her reservation was for one night only.

Seven came and went. Mariah waited until eight, then donned her wetsuit. She grabbed her bag and left through the airlock.

As soon as she surfaced, she could see that something was wrong. The cute little house out by the dock was covered in black scorch marks, and several of its windows had shattered. *A fire?* Mariah wondered. The owners had seemed like such nice people, and she hoped they were okay. She kicked off her flippers and ran into the house.

The house looked like it had suffered from some sort of disaster, but Mariah couldn't identify what kind. More random burn marks covered the walls, a lot of the glass items were broken, and some knickknacks had fallen off their shelves. Mariah called out, but no one answered. She made her way through the house, carefully sidestepping glass shards in her bare feet. She climbed over a fallen bookcase and opened the door to the bedroom.

The hosts – a man and a woman in their early forties – lay in bed, their bodies contorted in unnatural positions. Mariah didn't have to get any closer to know they were dead. The look on the man's face was that of extreme pain, and his skin was covered in burns. The woman's head was turned too far, and it was painful to look at.

Mariah shut the door and left the house. She had to sit

down for a minute. It was all just too much. When she could stand again, she removed her wetsuit and put on her jeans, a T-shirt, and some tennis shoes. She'd need to call someone. She rooted through her bag until she found her cell phone. No service. *What happened here?* she wondered.

Her rental car was parked outside. It also had some rough spots on the paint, and two of the windows were busted. Mariah brushed some glass off the driver's seat and attempted to start the car. It wouldn't start; it just made a clicking sound when she turned the key. She didn't know much about cars, but her guess was that it had a bad battery.

She went back into the house and poked around until she found the host's keys. Then she tried their car, but it wouldn't start either. *I don't like this*, Mariah thought. The site was pretty isolated, but Mariah remembered seeing a gas station not too far away. It would be a twenty-minute walk at most. Not seeing any other options, she began her hike.

Those mysterious scorch marks were all over the place. Black streaks marred the highway. Some of the palm trees were partially burned, and a few had even fallen over. The patterns made Mariah think of lightning, but how had there been so much of it? The skies hadn't even been cloudy when she'd gone into the water the previous day.

No cars passed her as she walked. She didn't remember it being a busy highway, but there should have at least been one by now. Up ahead she spotted a glimmer of light, just off the side of the road. She picked up her pace. A vehicle had gone over the embankment and now rested at a forty-five-degree angle. As she got closer, she saw that it was a blue minivan, marred by the same scorch marks she'd seen elsewhere. The driver and passengers were dead, looking just like the owners of SeaDreams. Mariah's heart broke when she saw the children in the backseat, their joints bent at disturbing angles.

She wanted to put the minivan behind her, but it had

something she needed. There was a bike rack on the roof, with two bikes attached. One of them appeared to be damaged, but the other one looked fine. They were bolted on, but Mariah kept a little toolkit in her backpack. Soon she was back on the road, making much quicker headway.

Smoke rose in the distance. She knew right away it would be the gas station. She passed two more wrecked cars before she reached it. There had been an explosion at the pumps, but it had since burned itself out. All the glass had broken in the storefront. It was dark inside, lit only by the sunlight from outside. The floor was covered with items that had fallen off the shelves. Some of the potato chip bags appeared to have exploded, and chips were everywhere.

Mariah grabbed a couple of water bottles and some snacks, then got back on her bike.

It was another half hour before she reached an actual town. She passed a bunch of businesses, most of which had broken windows. The same scorch marks were still everywhere, and a couple of the buildings were on fire. She didn't see any more bodies, though, except for those in wrecked cars. Whatever happened, appeared to have happened in the middle of the night, when fewer people were out.

Occasionally she'd call out, "Is anyone there?" Her words just echoed back to her. It now occurred to her that she hadn't seen any animals yet, either, except for a few dead birds on the road. She rode on until the businesses gave way to neighborhoods. She spent the majority of her day riding up and down each street, calling for help. No one answered.

When the sun started to set, she picked a house and went inside. Again she called out to see if anyone was inside, and again she got no answer. She poked her head into every room. There were corpses in the bedroom, so she kept that door closed. In the kitchen, she went through the pantry and made herself a peanut butter sandwich.

As she chewed, she mused that this might be one of the last times she got to eat bread. If this truly was an apocalypse, then the bread that was out there was all the bread that would ever be made. When it all went moldy in a few weeks, bread would go extinct, unless Mariah learned how to make it herself.

That's when she started crying. Now that she'd had the chance to sit down for a minute, the enormity of the day overcame her. She put down the rest of her sandwich and moved into the living room. Then she sat down on the couch and stared into space.

Was the entire world like this? Were there any other survivors? And of course the biggest question, just what the hell happened?

She reached into her backpack and retrieved her cell phone. Still no signal, and no wi-fi connections. The phone's battery was at sixty-seven percent, with no way to charge it.

She thought of an old Twilight Zone episode, the one where the guy breaks his glasses at the end. She wondered if she could find happiness in a world with no other humans, with only books for comfort. She doubted it. Books would only remind her of the world that once was. She no longer cared how many obstacles her favorite fictional characters overcame. They were all doomed anyway. The world ended in 2024, and none of these literary heroes could stop it. Their exploits had been rendered pointless.

Mariah did not want to remain in a world without other people. But before she started pursuing that line of thought, she had to be sure. She needed to know whether the entire world was gone, or just this city. She needed to know if anyone else had survived. And of course, she needed to know that this entire day hadn't just been a bad dream.

All things considered, she thought she'd have trouble falling asleep, but she didn't. A full day of bike riding and screaming herself hoarse had drained everything she had.

She curled up on the couch, closed her eyes, and was out like a light.

She woke up at dawn, packed up a few things, and rode north. When she got hungry, she stopped at a grocery store. It was in just as bad a shape as everywhere else, but the shelves were still stocked. Mariah had half-expected the place to be looted clean, but of course, that would have required other survivors. She grabbed some cans of meat and vegetables. She'd taken a can opener and some silverware from the house she'd slept in, and now she used them to eat a quick breakfast.

It occurred to her that if she really was the only survivor, she'd never have to worry about running out of food. The cans in one grocery store could keep her filled for years, and if not, she could always raid all the kitchens in a given neighborhood. Granted, even canned food expired eventually, but she had plenty of time to learn how to grow food of her own. Including bread.

But she didn't plan to stay in one place just yet. Not until she knew what was going on; not until she was sure she was alone. Her mission now was to find just one other person. Then she could think of settling down and learning to farm.

She visited a new city every few days, exploring as many neighborhoods as she could before the sun went down. She checked her phone again every few miles, hoping to find a signal. When her phone ran out of charge, she found a solar-powered charger at an electronics store. She also found a flashlight with a solar cell. She had to check eight boxes before she found one that still worked, as most of the store's electronics had been shorted out in what Mariah thought of as "the Event."

She attached both the charger and the flashlight to the outside of her backpack, so they could soak up the sun's rays as she traveled.

Nearly a month after the Event, Mariah was riding her bike through a neighborhood when she heard a man's voice shout, "Hey you!" She was so startled she fell off her bike. As she got to her knees, she heard footsteps running towards her. For a second her instincts told her to run, but her rational mind took over. Even if this stranger turned out to be a psycho killer, what did Mariah have to lose?

It was a man in his mid-twenties, with dark hair and a scraggly beard. "Oh my god," he said, as he helped Mariah to her feet. "You're real. You're really real." He hugged her hard, and she hugged back.

"I'm Mariah," she said.

"I'm Jared," he replied. They just stared at each other for a few minutes. They both had so many questions, that they couldn't speak at all. It was like a traffic jam of words blocking their mouths. Finally Jared managed to find his tongue. "Do you know what killed everyone?"

Mariah shook her head. "I was underwater at the time."

"I was lucky. I sleep in the basement. But there's also a sub-basement, that used to be a wine cellar before my parents turned it into a bathroom for me. I got up in the middle of the night to pee, and I saw these flashes of light around the door. When I got out, my TV had exploded, and there were shards of glass all over the floor. So I was in my bare feet like John McClane, and—"

"What do you think it was?" Mariah asked.

Jared shrugged. "Seemed like lightning? At first I thought it was a bad storm. But it killed everyone, I mean *everyone* in town. And there wasn't any rain."

They walked as they talked, Mariah pushing her bicycle. They found a bench and sat down.

"Could it be a weapon?" Mariah asked.

"Straight out of sci-fi if it was," Jared said. "Maybe this is how the alien invaders sterilize a planet before they take over."

"Well, I can't say I've noticed any flying saucers overhead," Mariah replied.

"Any idea how widespread this is?" he asked.

"No," she replied. "I hope it's not the whole world. I just wouldn't be able to take that." She told him about all the towns she'd passed through. Jared's story was similar, though he'd spent a week in his own neighborhood before venturing out, so he hadn't come quite as far.

They ate a late lunch together, with food gathered from a nearby store. As Mariah had predicted, bread was getting hard to find, and most refrigerated food had long since spoiled. They had to settle for cans.

"So what do you do?" Jared asked through a mouthful of cold chicken and dumplings.

"I write travel articles," Mariah said. "I'm almost always out of town, visiting—"

"So you're not from Florida?" Jared asked, and Mariah shook her head.

"No, I have an apartment in upstate New York. I was only—"

"I have friends up there!" Jared said. "Online friends, I mean. Well, I did. I wonder if they're still alive."

While Mariah was overjoyed to have someone to talk to, Jared wouldn't have been her first choice. He interrupted her a lot, for one thing. Also, he was only three years younger than her, but sometimes he acted like a teenager. She learned that he'd dropped out of college and had been living in his parents' basement. She tried not to judge him for that. College wasn't for everyone, and it wasn't like college mattered now, in this post-disaster world. But Mariah got the impression that he hadn't learned anything from the experience. He still talked like he expected someone to take care of him.

Still, he was another living human, and he could lift heavy things. If the dead started to rise or became radioactive mutants, Mariah felt safer at Jared's side than without him.

They traveled together for the next few weeks, still headed north, exploring a new town nearly every day. The corpses were starting to stink, so each time they found a house to stay in for the night, they'd wrap up the corpses in bedsheets and drag them outside. The vast majority of bodies they found were in bed. The Event had apparently happened quickly, without any warning. Maybe Jared was right about lightning, but how did the entire world get struck at once?

Neither of them wanted to sleep in a bed where a corpse had been rotting for two months, so they usually slept on couches or the occasional guest bed. They slept in separate rooms when possible. Mariah said it was because she needed her privacy, but the truth was, there was something about Jared she didn't trust.

They gradually found more working electronics, various solar-powered devices and chargers. They checked for cell signals and wi-fi every day, but never found any. Now and then they tried to get a car working, but to no avail. Something about the Event had fried every alternator, and neither Jared nor Mariah knew much about cars. Sooner or later they planned to find a book about car repair, but for now they were happy using bikes. Sure they were slower, but they had no reason to hurry. It wasn't as if they had a destination.

One night after dinner, they hooked up a portable DVD player to one of their power banks. They weren't sure if it would have enough power to watch an entire movie, but it was just for fun anyway. Halfway through the movie, Jared yawned and put his arm around Mariah. She was a little annoyed, but she didn't say anything at first. Then, twenty minutes later, he leaned in for a kiss.

Mariah held up her hand, pushing his face away. "Not

gonna happen, Romeo."

Jared took his arm off her shoulder, then crossed his arms and pouted. He was quiet for the rest of the movie.

He didn't speak again until they were about to go to bed. "Why not?" he asked.

Even though it had been a couple of hours, Mariah knew what he meant. "I just don't feel that way about you," she said.

"But I'm the last man on Earth," he said.

"I like girls," Mariah said. She'd already told him that a couple of weeks earlier. He'd seemed okay with it at the time.

"There aren't any girls," Jared said.

"So?" Mariah asked. "Doesn't mean I have to start liking guys."

"Can't you just… try it?" Jared asked.

"I have," Mariah said. "It wasn't for me."

"Maybe it's about the right guy," he said.

"Maybe it's about time you let it go," Mariah said.

"But this could be a fantasy world," Jared said. "For both of us."

"I'm so sorry this apocalypse isn't living up to your fantasies," Mariah said. "It's almost as if it's an actual tragedy, and not just the universe trying to help you get laid."

"I don't mean it that way," Jared said. "I just meant we can turn this hell into heaven. It's up to us to make life worth living again. Besides, it's our responsibility to repopulate the Earth."

"Gross," Mariah said, shaking her head. "You're not going to whine your way into bed with me. Good night."

The house had three bedrooms, and two of them had been unoccupied. It was a rare occasion when both of them could sleep in actual beds, instead of one having to settle for a couch.

No sooner had Mariah closed her eyes, when the walls started to shake. She heard a rhythmic thumping from the other side of the wall. *What in the world is he... oh*, Mariah thought. She rolled her eyes. She didn't care if he masturbated, that was his business. But given the conversation they'd just had, and the amount the room was shaking, she was sure he was making that much noise on purpose. He probably hoped it would make her feel guilty.

That's it, we're going to start sleeping in separate houses, Mariah thought. She wrapped her pillow around her ears and tried to go to sleep.

Neither of them spoke about the incident, but they were pretty cold towards each other for the next few days. But they really did need each other, and soon they were back to their normal routine. Or Mariah thought they were.

"All I'm saying is that the bacon biscuit should have cost less than the sausage one," Jared said.

"Uh huh," Mariah said, not really listening.

"It's just not as filling," Jared said, oblivious to her lack of interest. "You put bacon on a burger, and it's just a topping. But you put it on a biscuit, and suddenly it's the meat."

"Preaching to the choir," Mariah said flatly, staring at a window cling. They were sitting outside a fast food restaurant, eating shortbread cookies that were meant to be packaged with kid's meals. The cookies were shaped like clowns and anthropomorphic animals.

"You're using me, you know," Jared said, out of the blue.

"Hmmm?" Mariah asked, biting the head off a fast food mascot.

"You need me more than I need you," he said. "You take advantage of my muscles all the time. What do you bring to the party?"

"If that's really how you feel, take off," Mariah said. "I'll get by."

"I just think I should get something for all my hard work," he said.

Mariah sighed. "Like what," she said, looking him in the

eye. She didn't phrase it like a question, because she already knew the answer.

"You know what," Jared said.

"Grow up," Mariah said. "I'm sorry I'm not the sex doll you always imagined spending the apocalypse with. But if you can't learn to live with that, we should go our separate ways."

"Maybe we should," he said.

"Fine," Mariah said, standing up. "See you around."

She started to walk toward her bike, but Jared grabbed her arm. "Wait," he said.

Mariah turned toward him, her eyes shooting daggers. "What?"

His eyes were wide now, and he looked like he was on the verge of tears. "I'm sorry," he said. "I mean it, I'm sorry. Please don't go. I can't live without you."

"Will you stop coming onto me?" Mariah asked.

"I promise," Jared said.

"This is your last chance," Mariah said. "I mean it. Make me feel uncomfortable again, and I'm out of here."

"I promise," Jared repeated. "I'll... respect your boundaries."

And he kept that promise for nearly a week.

In her dream, Mariah lived in an underwater house. It wasn't a steel pod like the SeaDreams hotel, but a traditional, two-story suburban home, that just happened to be underwater. The entire neighborhood was submerged, but the rest of the houses held only corpses. Mariah stood on the sidewalk in front of her home, somehow still able to breathe, and looked up and down her street. In every home, corpses stood at their windows, staring at her with wide, judging eyes. What she had done to offend them, Mariah had no idea.

And then the octopus came. She wasn't sure where it had come from; she hadn't seen it swimming towards her. It was just suddenly in her face, its tentacles wrapped around her body, grabbing, reaching, keeping her from moving. One tentacle closed over her mouth, its suckers puckering against her face.

She woke to find Jared on top of her, one hand on her shoulder, the other on her left breast, his lips pressed hard against hers.

"Off!" she screamed, turning her head to the side. He grabbed her by the chin and turned her head back. It felt like he had at least six hands.

"Just try it!" Jared said, and leaned in again.

She could feel his erection against her thigh, and she started to panic. She beat on his shoulder with her free hand, but he didn't even seem to feel it.

Then she remembered something she'd heard back in college. She reached for his face and thrust her thumb under his eyelid.

"Yah!" he shouted, slapping her hand away. He put both hands on his face and started cursing up a storm.

Mariah's hands were free, but she was still pinned by Jared's weight. She reached beside the bed, looking for anything she could use as a weapon. All she could find was her flashlight.

Jared recovered and put both hands around her neck. As he started choking her, Mariah hit him in the nose with the flashlight. She heard a satisfying crunch, and Jared screamed in pain. Once again he let go of her so he could grab his face. Blood dribbled down his chin.

While he was distracted, Mariah managed to work a leg free, and she kicked him in the stomach. He started to reach for her again, but she kept kicking him until he took his weight off of her. Then she rolled out of the bed and ran.

She was barefoot, and even though it was early morning, the pavement was already hot. A few seconds after she ran out the door, she heard it slam again. Jared's footsteps pounded after her, and he was screaming a stream of nearly-unintelligible words, mostly variations of bitch and whore.

Mariah was a fast runner, but so was Jared. She knew that if he persisted, he'd catch up to her eventually. He was too close behind for her to find a place to hide. All she could hope for was that she'd outlast his tantrum. Once he calmed down a little, maybe he'd lose interest in the pursuit. But she wouldn't bet on it.

They ran for three blocks. All the while, Mariah scanned ahead for anything she might use as a weapon. A discarded baseball bat, a metal pipe, anything. But so far it had just been empty sidewalks and overgrown lawns.

She was starting to lose hope. He wasn't slowing down, and his curses were getting even more creative. If she stumbled, he'd be on her in an instant. What was he going to do when he caught her? She tried not to think about it. She wanted to know how close he was, but she couldn't take a look without slowing down.

There was a bang, and Jared cried out. The cursing stopped, and she no longer heard his footfalls. Had he run into a parked car? She wasn't ready to stop yet, though. It could have been a trick, though she wasn't sure how he'd made that noise.

She ran another half a block, then risked turning her head. He was no longer after her. Mariah slowed to a stop, then turned around. He lay on the hot pavement, completely still. She didn't want to get any closer, but curiosity got the better of her. When she was about twenty feet away, she spotted the blood. Jared didn't appear to be breathing.

Gunshot? Mariah looked around, instinctually raising her hands in surrender.

"Over here!" It was a woman's voice. It was hard to find the source at first, but then she spotted her. A woman was standing on a second-floor balcony, holding a rifle with a very large scope.

Mariah kept her arms raised as she approached. The

woman went back into her house, then emerged from her front door a minute later. She was dressed in military fatigues, and had short, blond hair. She'd left the rifle in the house. "Are you okay?" the woman asked, as Mariah reached her front steps. "I didn't mean to scare you."

"Thank you," Mariah said, hugging the stranger. "I'm Mariah," she said through sobs.

"Susan," the woman said, returning the hug.

"Any idea what killed everyone?" Mariah asked. The two sat on Susan's deck, taking a rest after disposing of Jared's body. They'd clicked instantly, despite the grisly work. In a strange way, Mariah felt like she was talking to an old friend.

"I doubt I know much more than you do," Susan said. "A couple of months ago, at around two AM, I was organizing my survival bunker when my radio started playing static. Assuming the worst, I sealed the door. Since then, I've been living in the bunker and trying to pick up radio signals. I only came out this morning because I found one."

"You did? What did it say?" Mariah asked.

"I didn't hear all of it," Susan replied. "But it said that the danger was over, and that if anyone was alive, they should head for the Pineapple Grove Mall. It's just a few miles from here. I was starting to pack up my things when I heard your 'friend' yelling at you."

Mariah sat up straight. "We should probably get going, then."

Susan nodded. "As soon as we're ready. But I want to make sure we're prepared for anything. This kind of crisis brings out the worst in some people, as you've just seen."

"I understand," Mariah said, thinking about Jared. From the moment he'd laid eyes on her, he'd seen the apocalypse as an opportunity. It had been a dream come true for him, a chance to do whatever he wanted with no repercussions. She wondered how many other survivors would have the same mindset.

They decided to wait one more day, during which Mariah's new friend showed her how to use a handgun, and the two of them packed a couple of backpacks with supplies.

That night, they slept in the same bed. For the first time since the Event, Mariah actually felt safe. She didn't know what surprises tomorrow would bring, but at least they had a direction. As she drifted off to sleep, her fears melted away, replaced by cautious optimism.

One way or another, they'd get through this. Together.

Third Shift

"Nothing is ever unoccupied," Mage said. "At least, not for more than a few minutes."

"What are you babbling about?" Trice asked, barely looking up from her phone.

"You leave a space, the air moves in to where you were," Mage said. "Simple physics, right?"

"Sure," Trice said. "So?"

"So what if it's not just air that rushes in?" Mage asked. "What if... *other things* are waiting to use that space, standing in a cosmic line, just waiting for you to get your ass out of the way?"

"I don't follow," Trice said. "What things?"

"Things we're not supposed to know about," Mage said, staring out the window.

"If you have time to squee, you have time to key," Mage said, rolling their eyes at the office gossips. The coworkers ignored them and continued gushing about the upcoming baby shower. *I'm going to be here all night,* Mage thought, typing furiously on their keyboard.

Since Mage was the only salaried employee in the department, they often ended up staying late to finish up paperwork. They didn't actually mind so much, as the office was so much more peaceful with their coworkers gone.

Without the distractions, Mage rarely had to stay more than an extra hour. It meant they got to miss five o'clock traffic, and it wasn't like they had a lot going on at home to get back to.

It was still unfair, though. The other office workers knew Mage would finish what they didn't, but they continued to chat when they should have been keying. That was office life. *Only thirty more years of this crap and I can retire,* Mage thought. It all felt like such a waste of time. They spent nearly fifty hours a week at work, leaving barely enough time in the day to eat, much less catch up on hobbies. The weekends were a blur, giving them just enough time to recover before Monday rolled around again.

Is this all life is? Mage wondered. *A repeating cycle of work? And when I finally retire, I'll be too old and broken to make the most of my free time. If I even live that long.* They felt like they were missing the best years of their life, always stuck behind a keyboard.

Their coworkers left at five o'clock sharp, but Mage kept on working. It was well after seven when they finally finished up. The office was eerily quiet, except for when the building settled. Sometimes Mage could swear they heard someone walking on the roof. The occasional creak sounded from down the hallway, but when Mage went to do the final walk around, no one was there. Mage was definitely alone.

With the final document filed, Mage gathered up their things, locked up the building, walked across the parking lot, opened their car door, and then remembered they'd forgotten their phone. With a heavy sigh, they turned around and headed back into the building. They passed the empty front desk, then walked back into the office area.

The room was full of people. Not just any people, but oddly misshapen people with bald heads and light purple skin. They appeared to have been in the middle of a conversation when Mage arrived. They had echoing voices consisting of creaks and whispers, as if the sounds of the building settling had coalesced into a language. Then the talking stopped and all eyes turned Mage's way.

One of the strange people stepped forward. His eyes were different sizes, and one was higher than the other. One of his nostrils was slitted, while the other was large and round. His mouth was on his left cheek. A jumble of Picasso paintings flashed through Mage's mind.

"You're going to forget you ever saw us," the purple man said. His voice was both deep and high-pitched, like two people talking at once. His larger eye, which was round and bulbous, quivered and glowed. Mage felt a weird tingling in their mind, and for a second, their brain felt lighter.

Then the strange people vanished. There was a mild rush of air, and the room felt a little cooler. Mage continued to their desk, picked up their phone, and walked back to the lobby. They hesitated by the front door, listening. They waited to see if there was another change in the air, or if those otherworldly voices resumed. But they didn't want to stand there too long, or the unusual visitors might guess why.

Mage wasn't sure what would happen then.

On the drive home, Mage realized they were sweating. It was the third time this year that they'd seen the "Other People," and probably the tenth or twelfth time in their life. They'd only been eleven years old the first time. The memory was still vivid. They'd gone to school on a Saturday - they could no longer remember why, they'd probably just been bored. They'd been surprised to find the door unlocked, but even more surprised to see classes in session. Purple teachers teaching purple children.

When the strange beings spotted Mage, they'd said nearly the same thing then that they said today. "You will forget you saw this." Mage had felt the same tingling, then turned and left the building.

But they hadn't forgotten.

Did others go through this? Did everyone stumble upon

these people eventually, after going somewhere they weren't supposed to be? Did the other humans actually forget, or, like Mage, were they just acting the part? Mage was afraid to find out what would happen if these Other People knew their demand hadn't worked.

What if Mage was the only human who could remember the Other People existed? Surely these creatures wouldn't let them live. And yet, the Other People didn't seem particularly hostile, just… private. Then again, thousands of people went missing every year, it's possible these beings were responsible.

Were they all over the planet? Did they just appear anytime someone left a room, or did they schedule their third-shift activities in places they knew would be unoccupied? It was the second time Mage had caught them in the office after hours, so it was likely that they knew it was a place they could expect twelve hours of privacy.

Where did they go when they were gone? Off to their home dimension? Or was Earth their home as well? Maybe they just teleported to the other side of the planet, to occupy the empty offices there.

It was a little weird that humans complained so much about space, and yet left so many buildings empty at night. In a more efficient world, when one set of office workers went home for the day, another shift would show up to work throughout the night. Granted, some businesses did work that way. Twenty-four-hour businesses probably never got visited by the Other People.

Mage didn't feel like the Other People wished them harm. And yet, driving home past dozens of other office buildings, and knowing that they might be filled with these otherworldly beings right now… The thought made their skin crawl.

Mage wanted to tell someone, but they didn't want to put someone else in danger. If these beings were vindictive, or even just paranoid, then Mage's knowledge could jeopardize anyone they told.

And yet, it was statistically unlikely that Mage was the only one who could remember them. If there were others like Mage out there, they wanted to meet them. But how could they find them without getting noticed? They weren't about to search for "Do you see purple people" on the internet. Those searches would be traced, and the Other People would know Mage could remember them.

Of course, it was also perfectly possible that Mage just suffered from hallucinations. They'd considered telling a psychologist, but again, danger.

Mage drove on, warily eyeing every dark building they passed, wondering which ones were truly empty.

"Can I stay here tonight?"

"Mage, I like you, but I don't think we're there yet," Trice answered.

"Not like that," Mage said. "I just… feel weird about going home."

"What's bothering you? You've been jumpy all night."

"Have you ever seen…" Mage paused, then lowered their voice. "…purple people?"

"Is that a band?" Trice asked.

"No," Mage said. "I mean actual… you know what? Never mind. If you had, you'd know."

"Go home," Trice said. "Get some rest. When you want to talk about what's bothering you, I'll be ready to listen."

Mage couldn't sleep. Every window made them nervous, like someone might be peeking in. They had to close all the shades before they felt comfortable, even though they lived on the third floor. Even then, they kept wondering if someone was in the next room. As they went from room to room, they knocked on each door frame, then waited a couple of seconds to give any potential visitors time to disappear.

On their third attempt to stay in bed, they came very close to finally passing out. They could feel the warm darkness closing in on the corners of their consciousness, ready to envelop their mind and block out the worries of the day. But before that warmth could spread too far, Mage felt the hair rise on their arm. Something changed in the room, something indefinable but unmistakable. There weren't any new sounds, the temperature hadn't changed, and the air was as calm as it had been before. There had been no vibrations, nothing to indicate someone had entered the room.

And yet Mage was one hundred percent sure that if they were to open their eyes right then, they'd see someone standing at the foot of their bed, staring at them. They lay there for half an hour, waiting for the feeling to go away, too afraid to sleep and too afraid to get up.

And then it was morning. Mage wasn't sure how they'd ever managed to get to sleep, but they felt well-rested. The sunlight chased away that feeling of dread, and Mage chastised themself for freaking out so much.

But the memories remained. The incident at the office, it *had* happened. As had all the previous encounters. Maybe they were hallucinations, but Mage remembered them as clearly as they remembered their college graduation, the camping trip they'd taken last year, and their mother's funeral.

It was Saturday, so Mage didn't have anywhere they had to be. Feeling emboldened by the rays of light coming through their windows, they decided to do some research. What had seemed risky the night before, now felt less dangerous.

Mage opened their laptop and loaded up their internet browser. Then they opened up a new tab in incognito mode. They started to type something into the search bar, but changed their mind. Then they downloaded a different browser, one that guaranteed privacy. Once again, they paused.

If I'm going to do this, I'm going to do it right, Mage thought.

They signed up for a thirty-day free trial of "CleanBrowse VPN," a software suite that advertised absolute privacy online. Only then did Mage feel comfortable enough to type what they wanted into the search bar.

They started by typing "purple people" into the search engine. The top results included a children's book, an Italian protest movement, and a popular novelty song from 1958. Then they typed, "Has anyone seen purple people?" That still didn't yield any useful results. They began typing more specific queries, such as "people who appear in empty rooms" and "creatures who occupy buildings after hours." They also described the people in more detail, mentioning their strange facial features and their ability to make people forget.

As they got deeper into the searches, they started to find more relevant search results. However, whenever they clicked a promising link, they would get 404 errors or pages that read, "This site no longer exists."

Each of the search results had a small preview, just a sentence or two, of the text that would have appeared on the page. These snippets alone were enough to prove Mage wasn't alone. Other people had seen these things. But there was no way to view the web pages.

They searched for "how to view web pages that no longer exist," and were directed to a site that archived a lot of internet content. However, the websites Mage needed had been purged from that site as well.

There was a tiny movement in the reflections on the laptop's screen, and Mage thought they heard someone exhale. They quickly turned around, but no one was there. When they turned back to the laptop, the text in the search bar read, "Let it go."

Mage shivered and could feel the hair standing up on the back of their neck. They shut the laptop and took a break.

* * *

Mage spent the day jumping at shadows. They drove out to the nearest drugstore to buy some sleeping pills. While there, they kept thinking they saw purple out of the corner of their eye, but no one was there when they turned their head. At one point they glanced up at the security mirror that hung above the aisles. For just a second they thought they saw someone standing behind them. But after they blinked, Mage stood alone.

They took the pills before bedtime and fell asleep much faster than they had the night before. Unfortunately, the pills wore off after about four hours, at which point they were wide awake. They got up to use the restroom, and they could have sworn the living room light turned off right as they opened the bedroom door.

After Mage got into bed and closed their eyes, once again they thought they felt a presence in the room. They took a couple of deep breaths and tried to think of something else. Some hobby they enjoyed, someone they liked talking to. Trice. Her face entered their mind, and it calmed them down. They decided they'd go see her Sunday evening if she wasn't busy. They started picking out a movie to suggest.

There was a creak, and Trice vanished from their mind. Buildings creaked, it didn't mean there were people in the room. Or maybe buildings didn't actually settle, and that was something humans had made up to explain all the creaks and groans they heard all night. Maybe all creaks were actually the Other People.

They heard another soft creak, but this time Mage thought they heard their name. Except they didn't literally hear the word "Mage." It was more like they suddenly knew that the creaking sound translated into "Mage," in the same way people made a "Hmmm?" sound to mean "What did you say?"

What do I even mean by that? Mage thought. It was a crazy notion. Insane. And yet, for the rest of the night, whenever Mage heard another squeak, creak, or groan from the walls, they felt like someone was calling them.

* * *

Sunday morning they called Trice and asked if they could see her that evening. She had trouble understanding what Mage was saying and had them repeat themself multiple times during the phone call. "Sorry, it must be a bad connection," Mage said. Which was odd, because they could hear her just fine.

Trice agreed to see them, and Mage spent the next hour trying to decide what movie to suggest they watch. She usually appreciated their taste in movies, and some of Mage's favorite films were now Trice's favorites as well. Mage looked through the DVDs on their shelves, but nothing jumped out at them. Then they loaded up a streaming app and started scrolling through the titles.

Not a single plot seemed interesting. It was as if Mage's passion for movies was still asleep. Mage remembered how after their mother died, nothing seemed fun for a few weeks. This was the same, except Mage wasn't grieving. Sure, they were a little worried about their mental state, but there was no reason they shouldn't be able to enjoy a movie.

The streaming menu currently highlighted a superhero movie. Mage had stopped it halfway through last time, and out of curiosity, they hit resume. The brightly-clad hero was fighting a villain in black armor. Citizens ran for their lives as the two threw each other into building after building, their fracas threatening to turn the city into rubble.

Mage had seen the movie seven times and had found themself invested every time. But now? They didn't really care who won. They didn't care if the innocent bystanders survived. It was like watching two insects fight. It was mildly interesting in a nature documentary sort of way, but if a giant boot were to smash both contestants flat, it would have been the same to Mage.

In fact, the more Mage watched, the more they lost track of who the hero was. Their motivations were distant and hard to follow. The man in the brightly-colored spandex wanted to save the other humans. But those humans would only live another hundred years or so anyway, so what was the point? When life was measured in such a blink of an eye, did a few extra decades even matter?

Meanwhile, the armored guy wanted to rebuild the world so that there would be no more war or poverty. Sure, it came at the cost of a few freedoms, but in the end, the planet would be a more peaceful place.

Still, neither side followed the Sti'Chu'Lek way. That was the way of true peace. Only use what wasn't in use. Only watch, never interfere. Leave no trace, no memory of your presence.

Mage had drifted off, but now they shook themself awake. The *what* way? Where had those thoughts even come from?

It was already dark outside. The streaming service had autoplayed the next four movies in the series, and Mage had missed most of their Sunday. They needed to see Trice right now.

They ran to the bathroom to fix their hair. In the mirror, their skin was an odd color, a much deeper pink, almost bordering on *don't say it don't think it don't acknowledge it* but maybe they were just coming down with something. One of their eyes was swollen too. Probably an allergic reaction. Trice was a nurse, she would know what to do.

They were still in their pajamas, but they didn't notice or care. Human clothing was so arbitrary. Cloth was cloth, why did they obsess about it so much? They ran down the stairs, got in the car, started the engine, and drove away.

They had to readjust their seat while driving. They couldn't tell if they'd grown or shrunk, but they were no longer comfortable in the car seat. They undid their seatbelt, ignoring the warning beep. They couldn't see out the rearview mirror anymore. They adjusted the mirror, only to see a mismatched set of eyes staring at them from the backseat.

Two nights earlier, when Mage had seen the Other People

at the office, they'd all looked alike to them. But this time, Mage immediately recognized the creature in their back seat. It was the same Sti'Chu'Lek who had asked them to forget. And somehow, on some level, they could feel the being's presence, and they knew it was the same presence they'd felt in their apartment the last couple of days.

Mage wasn't afraid. They didn't panic or hit the brakes, they just kept driving at a steady pace. It took them a few seconds to find their tongue, and they asked, "What happens now?" As they said it, they realized that they were no longer speaking English.

"You either forget us or become us," the being said.

Mage understood. "I'm ready," they said.

Trice put down the phone, tears in her eyes. They'd found Mage's car wrapped around a telephone pole. No body had been recovered yet, but there was no way anyone could have survived such an accident.

She couldn't help but feel like it was her fault. They had been on the way to see her when they'd crashed. She'd probably never know what had caused Mage to lose control of the car. Engine trouble? Oil patch? Deer? She would wonder about that forever.

She thought she heard a noise from her bedroom and ran to look. The lights were off, but she saw the silhouette of a person standing by her bed. For just a moment, she thought it was Mage. They were the wrong height, and something seemed off about their limbs, but there was... *something* about the way they stood and moved. Something Mage-like.

"Who are you?" Trice asked. She flicked the light switch, but they didn't come on.

"Goodbye," the figure said, and vanished.

Trice blinked a couple of times, then felt a spot of dizziness. When she looked up again, she wondered why she was standing in the bedroom doorway. The last thing she remembered was being in the living room, and getting a distressing phone call. A friend of hers had died in a car wreck.

A good friend? Something more? Oddly, she couldn't remember. She could remember Mage's face – sort of – but she couldn't remember how she'd met them or whether they'd been close.

"I hope they found whatever peace they needed," she said out loud, then returned to the living room and started watching television. Something felt empty about the evening, like she was missing out on something she'd had planned. There was a half memory floating just above her consciousness, and try as she might, she couldn't grab onto it. *Oh well*, she thought. *If it's important, it'll come to me.*

From the darkness of Trice's kitchen, Mage took one last look at her. They hoped she would live a long, happy life, at least in human terms. When they were ready to go, they nodded to their mentor. The two blipped away, back into the Elsewhere.

Forever Home

A chill air swept through the bedroom. The couple slept soundly, oblivious to the change. Tendrils of darkness coalesced into long, wispy fingers. Above the bed, a pair of insubstantial hands flexed, finally realizing some semblance of form for the first time since the spirit's demise. An eye opened, then another. The ghostly eyes were gray and barely visible, but their tortured gaze held the pain of one who had suffered much in life.

No arms or head manifested to join the disembodied parts. The spirit had all it needed to interact with the world again. Propelled by curiosity, It touched the ceiling with one intangible fingertip. It couldn't feel the ceiling's texture, but it did note the change in temperature as it made contact.

No words crossed the spirit's mind. "Words" and "mind" were concepts beyond the creature's grasp, things that only mattered to the living. Still, in a rudimentary way, the spirit wanted to understand where it was and how it had come to be. It found no answers by touching the ceiling, and curiosity started to give over to sadness. Next it touched a wall, but once again found no answers within. The sadness morphed into impatience, and threatened to turn into anger.

The eyes settled on the two sleeping men, and the round mass of fur curled between them. It wanted to hurt them. It didn't know why. Whatever academic degrees the spirit might have held in its former life, that brain had long since rotted away, and all that was left was an incorporeal cloud of emotional energy. It didn't know jealousy from Swiss cheese, those were just words. All it knew was that those in the bed had something the spirit wanted. Life. As the haunting eyes glared at the men, a long-fingered hand reached toward them.

Lying between the men, the fluffy cat opened its eyes, uncurled, and moved into a sitting position. Staring directly into the spirit's eyes with a look of defiant boredom, the cat said, "No."

Now the spirit experienced a new emotion. Fear. It wasn't sure what it had to fear from this animal, but it didn't want to find out. As it recoiled, the hands dissipated, then the eyes, and the last bit of supernatural energy diffused into the air.

The cat stretched and yawned, then curled back into a ball and fell asleep.

"So this is how it works, kid," Pompom said, watching the black-and-white kitten bat a toy butterfly back and forth. "The humans feed us and keep the rain off our heads. But it's not for free. They need us as much as we need them, never forget that."

"This place is amazing," Spackle said. "So much bigger than the place with the cages." She'd just lost the butterfly under the couch, but now she spotted a catnip ball, and she moved into pounce position. The ball suspected nothing. Spackle launched herself forward with a bit too much force and tumbled forward with the ball between her paws.

"Pay attention," Pompom said. His long brown-and-black fur obscured his legs, and to Spackle, he looked like a living mountain of fur.

"I'm listening," Spackle said, now concentrating on a TV remote. It had been placed on the coffee table with one corner hanging over the side, and now it taunted Spackle, daring her to pull it to the floor. She jumped straight up three times, but couldn't quite reach it. Before she could try a fourth time, Pompom placed a paw on her head.

"It isn't always going to be playtime," Pompom warned her. "Sometimes the humans will be sad. It's our job to make them smile. Sometimes they don't get enough exercise. You'll have to make sure they play with you. Sometimes—"

"Where are the humans now?" Spackle asked, squirming out from under Pompom's massive paw.

"They're gone a lot during the day," Pompom said. "I assume it's to hunt, because sometimes they come back with food. But they—"

"What are they called?" Spackle asked. She'd spotted a scrap of paper and was going in for the kill.

"The taller one is called Geoff, and the one with no fur is called Allen," Pompom said.

Spackle giggled, nearly choking on the paper she was eating. "Humans have funny names," she said.

"Indeed," Pompom said. "As I was about to say, it is also our job to protect them."

"From what?" Spackle asked, spitting out the paper. "They're so big, what could possibly hurt them?"

"Bugs, mostly," Pompom answered. "They get in the house, we have to take them out. Rodents, too, but I haven't seen one in years. My reputation must have scared them off." He sat even more proudly.

"Anything else?" Spackle asked. She tried to pounce on Pompom but she just bounced off his fur.

"Yes," Pompom said dramatically. "The most important one of all. We must protect them from... the spirits."

Spackle stopped playing. She felt her fur rise slightly. Finally giving Pompom her full attention, she sat upright and asked the obvious question. "What are spirits?"

"They're what is left behind when a human passes... on," Pompom said, still injecting an air of ominousness into his words. "These spectral denizens of the night have been known to scare humans… to death."

"To death?" Spackle repeated, her eyes wide.

"Not while we're around," Pompom answered. "See, humans are afraid of spirits. But spirits are afraid of us. All we—"

"Why?" Spackle asked, looking up at Pompom with huge, inquisitive eyes. "Can we hurt them?"

"Yes and no," Pompom answered. "A spirit's only weapon is fear. It is also their only weakness. They feed on fear, but they fear what isn't afraid of them."

"But I am afraid," Spackle said. "They sound scary."

"You won't be afraid when you're older," Pompom said. "Until then, stay by my side."

"But how are you not scared?" Spackle asked.

"I'll teach you," Pompom said. "But the first step is to feel something else."

"Huh," Spackle said. Then something else occurred to her. "Does every house have a cat, then?" she asked.

"No, but not every house has a spirit," Pompom told her. "And some spirits are more dangerous than others. Some never gather the energy it takes to attack a human. But once a spirit senses fear, it's like tuna to them. They can't touch anything, and that frustrates them. Sure, they can throw energy around to bump objects off shelves, but they can't control it very well. Causing fear is the only way they can directly interact with the world. And then it becomes a vicious cycle. The fear makes them stronger, which makes them scarier, which causes more fear."

"So why don't we fear them?" Spackle asked.

"Because we can see them," Pompom said.

"The humans can't see them?" Spackle asked. "Then why do they fear them?"

"The humans can feel the spirit's energy in the room," Pompom said. "They can almost make out shapes in the darkness. They can see objects move. If anything, being invisible makes the spirit scarier. Think about it. If you thought there might be a rabid dog in the room, would you be more or less afraid if it was invisible?"

"Oh," Spackle said, but that gave her another thought. "Can dogs see spirits?"

"No, but they can smell them, and that's almost as good," Pompom said. Spackle had more questions, but Pompom cut her off. "You don't need to learn too much in one day," he told her. "There'll be time enough."

Spackle was asleep under the living room sofa when she thought she heard something scream. She blinked the sleep from her eyes, then crawled out from under the furniture. All the lights were off now, but she could see well enough. The earlier conversation had spooked her, and she anxiously perked up her ears for more cries.

She heard it again. It was coming from the kitchen, but it was faint. It was... a meow? She ran into the kitchen and looked around. "Pompom?" she asked.

"Over here," Pompom called. His voice came from the door to the basement. Spackle hadn't been down there yet.

"What are you doing in there?" Spackle asked through the door.

"I was asleep in the warm laundry and they must have shut the door," Pompom replied. "They used to keep this door open. I guess they closed it so you wouldn't fall down the stairs. I've been calling for an hour but I don't think they can hear me."

"I'm not surprised. I barely heard you myself," Spackle said.

"Listen, this is very important," Pompom said. "Go upstairs and wake them up. Try to get them to follow you downstairs."

"I'll try," Spackle said.

She ran back through the living room and over to the staircase. The steps were taller than she could leap. Luckily they were carpeted, so even though she wasn't big enough to bound up the steps like Pompom, she had no trouble climbing them one at a time. It took longer, and she was a bit out of breath when she reached the top, but she made it.

She zipped into the bedroom and was about to climb up the comforter when she spotted movement. Above the bed, something was moving. No, not just something. It was as if the darkness itself had come alive and formed a pair of elongated hands.

Spackle backed into the hallway. *Think, think, think,* she told herself. *What did Pompom say? Show no fear. But how do I do that when my heart is beating so fast?*

She thought about running back down to the kitchen and asking Pompom for advice. But if she did that, she'd never make it back up the stairs in time. She thought about meowing at the top of her lungs, to wake the humans up. Except that would also attract the attention of the spirit. But then, wasn't that what she wanted? To keep the spirit away from the humans?

She wasn't sure. *I can't wake the humans up,* she thought. *If they sense the spirit, they'll be afraid, and their fear will feed it.* But she was afraid too, and if she drew the spirit's attention toward her, it would feed just as easily.

It can't hurt me if I'm not afraid, she told herself. *But I am afraid, so that doesn't help a whole lot. What was it Pompom said? "The first step is to feel something else." What does that even mean?*

She watched the creature raise its hands. It was trying to touch the bed, but its fingers just passed right through it. It seemed frustrated and was working itself into a rage. It swept one hand aside, and a floor lamp fell over. One of the humans stopped snoring for a second but then went right back to sleep.

Perplexed by this new development, the spirit nudged the lamp again. Nothing happened. It tried a few more times, getting angrier each time until it successfully pushed it again. As Spackle watched, the spirit worked with the lamp, getting better and better until it was able to move the lamp at will.

Spackle was aghast. If this went on much longer, the spirit wouldn't even need anyone's fear. With this much control of its energy, it could strangle the humans in their sleep. And then what would happen to Pompom? Without the humans, Spackle wouldn't be able to free him from the basement. They could starve waiting for another human to visit.

And all because Spackle couldn't suppress her fear. She had failed her new humans. This nice, friendly couple had taken her away from the cold cages and given her a warm new home, and this is how she repaid them? She was mad at herself. She was mad at her fear. But most of all, she was mad at this spirit.

This newfound anger edged out her fear. How dare this spirit barge into the home of these nice people? What had the humans ever done to it? How dare it jeopardize Spackle's new forever home. It wasn't fair, and the spirit wasn't going to get away with it.

Spackle rushed into the bedroom, climbed up the comforter, and put on her meanest face. She scanned the darkness until she found what had to be the spirit's eyes. It looked at her with curiosity. The lamp fell back to the floor.

"Go away," the tiny kitten said, glaring into the spirit's eyes.

The spirit cringed for a moment, then recovered. It swiped one of its spectral hands, knocking Spackle back to the floor. Then, emboldened by the action, it seemed to grow in power. The hands became less ethereal, and its eyes turned from gray to white. And beneath those eyes, a wicked smile appeared in the darkness, spreading until it became a gaping maw full of long, black teeth.

Once again it reached for the sleeping couple. But Spackle was back, and this time she wasn't just angry, she was furious. She stood between the spirit and her humans, her back arched and her fur standing on end. She hissed and spat and growled, all the time fixing the spirit with her meanest glare.

The spirit took another swipe at her. To its surprise, its hand went right through the kitten without making contact. It tried again, then twice more, each time with the same outcome. The spirit's eyes filled with doubt, and it became less substantial. The kitten spat again, and the spirit diminished even more. The spirit became an ethereal mass of fear and doubt, the two emotions picking at each other until the spirit was nothing more than a pair of transparent gray eyes.

Spackle hissed one last time, then growled, "Never. Come. Back." The eyes vanished.

One of the humans, Allen, moaned in his sleep. Geoff rolled over and patted him on the shoulder. "Did you hear something?" Geoff asked.

"I think the kitten knocked over the lamp and it spooked her," Allen mumbled.

"Ah," Geoff said. He felt around with his hand, patting Pompom's usual spot. "Where's Pompom?" he asked.

"Dunno," Allen said. "It's laundry day so he's probably shedding on our clean clothes again... Shoot!"

"What?" Geoff asked, now fully awake.

"I closed the basement door," Allen said.

"I'll get it," Geoff said, climbing out of bed.

A few minutes later, all four household members were back in bed. Three of them were asleep again within minutes. Only Spackle remained awake, soothed by the rhythmic breathing of her bed companions. She padded around the bed until she found the perfect spot, nestled among the other three warm bodies. She stretched one last time before curling into a ball.

Spackle purred, calmed by feelings of belonging, safety, and pride. *I think I'm going to do all right here*, she thought just before she drifted off to sleep.

Dixieland

It started with a class field trip. Song and I sat together on the bus. We held hands, we talked, we were so in the moment, it was like the rest of the bus didn't even exist. I know she felt it too, I saw it in her eyes. Plus, no classes. It was such a pleasant ride that I was actually kind of bummed when the bus arrived at Rock City.

But the day got even better. The teachers didn't make us stay together, so we got to walk around at our own pace. While some of the other seniors ran up and down the path like it was a race, Song and I took it slow, enjoying the sights, the sun, and each other's company. We found a nice bench and sat down for a while, with our arms around each other's waists. When I thought the time was right, I leaned in for a kiss.

"Eww, PDA," a voice said. Eric, the class clown, stood in front of us, sneering. "Get a room, girls," he said. "No one wants to see that."

"I do, I do," shouted another guy who came running up. It was Eric's best friend, Abel. "Heck, I'll pay good money. How 'bout it, Rahima?"

I rolled my eyes. "Yeah, you better hold onto that money. You're going to need it to..." I paused. I couldn't think of a snarky enough way to end the sentence.

"...to pay your prom date," Song finished. That's why I

like her. If I drop the ball, she's always there to pick it up.

The guys laughed and moved on, and Song and I stood up and resumed walking. A few minutes later the path went into a cave. I removed my sunglasses and put them in my purse. Song and I held hands as we shuffled through the tunnel. On each side, waist-high alcoves were illuminated with neon lighting, to highlight the quartz and other pretty crystals. The crowd was a bit more dense in the cave, so walking was slower.

We soon found ourselves behind Eric and Abel again. Eric was showing off. He reached into an alcove and started touching the crystals.

"Dude, you're going to get us into trouble," Abel said.

"For touching a rock?" Eric asked. "Get real. Watch this." He reached far into one alcove, where a carrot-shaped stalactite hung from the ceiling. He grabbed it and started stroking it, moving his hand up and down in a decidedly lewd fashion. "Hey Abel, this remind you of one of your dates?"

"Now *that's* PDA," Song said. "You and that rock must have a very special relationship."

"Hey, I'm just getting my r—" Eric began, but then the stalactite broke off in his hand. "Shit!" he said, trying to get the rock to stick back to the ceiling. When that didn't work, he set it down in the alcove.

I ducked my head into the alcove, looking at the spot where the piece had broken off. There was a hole in the ceiling, and nothing but blackness inside. "Huh," I said. "It's hollow." I started to reach toward the hole.

"Do you hear something?" Abel asked.

I pulled my hand away, straining to hear. There was a buzzing sound, like being near a beehive. It was hard to tell, but it seemed like it was coming from the hole. And it was getting louder.

"I don't like this," Song said. "Can we move on?"

Suddenly a swarm of... insects? ...burst from the hole.

Song and I dropped to the floor as the air became thick with the locust-like creatures. All around us, people screamed and fled the cave. Someone stepped on my arm as they trampled over me. Song and I crawled toward the exit.

Ahead of me, Eric shrieked. The creatures swarmed all over him, covering his body from head to toe. Abel stood beside him, swatting at the things with his jacket, but that just got their attention. Soon they were on him too. I couldn't see them very well in the dark, but the bugs didn't look like any kind of insects I'd ever seen. They almost looked like little people. But I knew that had to be my imagination getting the better of me.

Song and I turned around and crawled in the opposite direction. "Ow!" Song shouted. "They bite!" We kept going. I could feel the things buzzing just above my hair, and I pulled my jacket up over my head. We finally made our way back into the daylight. People thrashed and screamed all around us, as swarms of the creatures randomly descended on them.

"Just run," I said, grabbing Song's hand tight. We didn't look back, we just ran at top speed through the rock-lined paths, thinking about nothing else until we burst through the exit gate and ran back to the bus. The bus driver, Mr. Davis, sat in the driver's seat, staring out the window with his mouth open. He opened the door as he saw us coming.

"Close it close it close it!" Song shouted as soon as we were on board. Four other students had beaten us onto the bus, and by their expressions, I could tell they were as freaked out as we were. Mr. Davis quickly shut the doors, right before the sky went black.

Thousands - maybe millions - of these things flew over and around the bus. Several of them landed on the windows, and I got a clear view of them for the first time. They looked like tiny women, each shorter than the length of my index finger, with dragonfly wings. But these fairies weren't like the ones I'd seen in cartoons. Their skin was gray, in some places decaying so that you could see patches of bone.

"Zombie fairies," I said out loud. On most days, that combination of words would have brought a laugh from someone nearby, but nobody laughed. The creatures pounded on the glass, but they were too weak to cause any damage. One by one they gave up in frustration, flying off to look for easier prey.

Through the dark swarm, we saw more figures approaching the bus. It was our teacher, Mrs. Henslow, and two students. They pushed their way through the swarm, determined to make it to the bus. They held their arms in front of their faces like they were navigating a raging snowstorm.

But then the swarm thickened around them until each of them wore a layer of fairies like it was the latest fashion trend. One by one the figures fell to the ground, waving their arms in panic. After a few seconds, they stopped moving. When the fairies finally dispersed, only their skeletons remained.

"Zombie fairies," I said again, mostly because I couldn't think of any other words. I heard a sobbing sound next to me. Song had her face buried in her hands. I put my arm over her shoulder, but I didn't say anything. I wanted to tell her everything would be okay, but I knew it would sound like a lie. We had a pact never to lie to each other.

I looked behind me. The other four students – Dmitrei, Eira, Greg, and Lea - stared back in shock. Lea's face had turned green, and as soon as I locked eyes with her, she fell to her knees and threw up. Greg stood up and ran to stand behind Mr. Davis. "Drive! Drive!" Greg yelled.

Mr. Davis had looked conflicted before, but that bit of encouragement was enough to get him moving. It didn't matter that Greg was just a student, with no authority to give any orders. Mr. Davis put the bus into gear and started driving like a madman.

I kept looking out the windows as he drove. The swarm

was everywhere. It fanned outward from Rock City, spreading in every direction, blotting out the sky in some places. How many of these things could there possibly be, all from that one hole? It just didn't seem possible. Granted, none of it seemed possible, but I'd like to think these magic flying piranha women followed at least *some* laws of physics.

The hole Eric made, did it lead to a cave? Or was it a portal to another dimension? Why did Eric have to be so dumb, anyway? Why couldn't he just… and then it hit me that Eric was probably dead now, along with Abel and dozens of other students. I never liked Eric, but I'd never wish *this* on him. I'd never…

I got dizzy. Song and I leaned on each other for the rest of the trip. We weren't sure where Mr. Davis was taking us, but anywhere was better than here. Or was it? With the speed at which these things were spreading across the sky, was anywhere safe? Would anywhere ever be safe again?

I'm not sure how long we rode. I think I slept for part of it. I'm not sure how I could have slept during such an ordeal, but honestly, I think my brain just couldn't handle everything that had happened. I was dimly aware of someone crying behind me, and occasionally someone - Lea, I assume – would throw up again.

Our phones all blared simultaneously, jolting me awake. The alert read: "Citywide Emergency – Stay In Your Homes – Watch Local News For More Details." Now that I was looking at my phone, it occurred to me to call mom. But when I hit the button, I got a message saying "Network Error – Systems Overloaded – Try Again Later."

I looked out the window. The sky was still dark, and cars were parked on the side of the road. Occasionally we'd pass another skeletonized corpse. I couldn't look anymore, and went back to my phone. I tried to pull up a news site but the internet was too slow. I put the phone back in my purse and rested my head against my girlfriend's.

Looking down at Song's hands, I noticed the bites for the first time. The edges of her wounds were starting to turn blueish-white, in stark contrast to her caramel-colored skin. A hundred zombie movies flashed through my mind. *No, I thought. Not now. Worry about it later.*

I realized we were on the street that led back to school. Of course, where else? With no other destination in mind, Mr. Davis was doing his job, driving the students back where they started. His brain was probably just as fried as mine was, and he was running on autopilot. Or maybe he just thought the school was the safest place to take us.

When we pulled up to the school, there were only a handful of cars in the parking lot. It was a half-day for those not on the field trip, so most of the students had gone home before the disaster started. Mr. Davis drove the bus up onto the sidewalk, getting us as close as he possibly could to the front door. Then he put the bus in park and called us over. Fairies still swarmed around the bus, some occasionally landing on the windows and scratching at the glass.

"The door's going to be locked," Mr. Davis said, pulling out his keys. He selected one of the keys and held it out to Dmitrei. "You'll go out first," he said. "Run straight for the door and unlock it. The rest of us will be right behind you."

"I can't do it," Lea said. She gestured toward the windows. "I can't run through that. I just can't."

"You have to be strong, Lea," Mr. Davis said. "It's just fifteen, maybe twenty feet. Just run. You'll be through before you know it."

She shook her head. "No," she said. "No no no no. I'll stay here. I'll be fine. Somebody will come for us."

Mr. Davis exhaled. "Okay, climb onto my back. Can you do that? Put your arms around my neck, and I'll get us there."

Lea still looked scared, but she nodded weakly. We all stood up, with Dmitrei in the front. Mr. Davis had obviously picked him for his strength. Dmitrei was on the football team, and built like it. If anyone could barge his way through the fairy swarm, it was him.

Mr. Davis put his hand on the door release, Lea now clinging to his back. When everyone was in place, he nodded and said, "All right, on three. One… two… three!" He pulled the handle, the door opened, and Dmitrei burst into the swarm. Eira was next, followed by Song and me, then Greg, and finally Mr. Davis and Lea.

Dmitrei reached the door and unlocked it, pulling it open. He probably should have gone on inside, but instead he held it open for the rest of us. I pushed ahead, following Eira into the building. I could barely see through the swarm, and had my jacket over my head anyway. I felt Greg's hands on my back, and he practically pushed me through the door.

The door slammed shut, which confused me. We couldn't possibly all be inside yet. I ran to the door and looked out the window. Lea and Mr. Davis had fallen, and Dmitrei had run over to help them. The swarm coalesced on the three of them, once again making them look like they were coated in fairies. The largest figure pulled Lea off the bus driver's back and tucked her under his arm, carrying her to the door as if she were a really large football.

I opened the door as he approached, and he tossed Lea through the door before collapsing. The door slammed shut again. I stood at the window, paralyzed with fear, as Dmitrei and Mr. Davis were consumed by the voracious undead fey. There was a commotion behind me, and I turned away from the carnage. A few of the fairies had gotten in with us, and the other students were swatting at them with whatever they had handy.

Eira managed to smack one with her purse, and it splatted against the wall like a large bug. The fairies weren't so tough taken one or two at a time. Within a couple of minutes, we had managed to kill most of them. A couple flew down the hall, turning the corner and buzzing out of sight.

We sat against the wall, breathing heavily. I looked around at my fellow students. There were now five of us – me, Song, Eira, Greg, and Lea. None of us said anything for a very long time. Finally Greg spoke up. "I need some water," he said, getting to his feet. This broke the bubble, and the rest of us stood as well.

Over the next few hours, we took stock of our needs. The electricity still worked. Cell services were still down. All the doors were locked, and none of the windows were broken. At least two fairies were loose in the building, but we couldn't find them. We retrieved some baseball bats from the gym, and we each carried one at all times. There was plenty of food in the cafeteria fridge, probably enough to feed us for weeks.

Song and Lea had suffered several fairy bites, and they were starting to feel sick. The school had a little room for sick students, with a couple of beds and a cabinet full of medical supplies. We put each of them on a bed and put antiseptic on their bites. Song's bites were starting to swell and had turned from light blue to nearly white. Lea's bites were still in the early stages.

As I tried to comfort Song, Greg tapped me on the shoulder. "Rahima, can I talk to you in the hall?" I followed him, leaving Eira alone with the two sick girls.

"What is it?" I asked.

"I think we should kill them," Greg whispered.

"What?" I asked.

"Keep your voice down," he said. "Seriously, have you ever seen a zombie movie? Lea and Song are going to turn against us, probably when we least expect it."

"We don't know that," I said. "We haven't seen any zombie humans yet. Who knows what their bites do to us?"

"Better safe than sorry," Greg said.

"You don't even have a way to do it," I told him. "What would you do, bash their heads in with a bat? Do you think you're even capable of that?"

"Actually I was thinking I'd use one of the poisonous chemicals in the science room," he said.

"Don't you dare," I said. "You try anything like that, and I'll…"

"Okay, okay," Greg said. "Keep your voice down. We'll just watch them for now. But if it looks like they're going to turn into zombies, you're not going to stop me."

I didn't say anything. I just turned around and went back in to see Song.

That night we grabbed some gym mats to sleep on. I didn't want to be far from Song, so I put my mat on the floor next to her cot. Greg and Eira probably would have done the same, but the room wasn't that big, so they slept on mats in the principal's office. I don't think any of us slept very much.

At three AM our phones beeped again, but it didn't have any new information. Just another warning to stay indoors. I tried calling my mom again, but cell service was still out. So I sent her a text. "I'm OK – at school." I got an error message when I tried to send it, but with any luck it would go out when the service came back up.

That made me wonder just how bad things were out there in the world. Anyone who was outdoors when it happened was probably toast. Same with anyone who had their windows open, whether in their car or their house. I wondered if these things could get through window screens.

Some people would have died trying to rescue others, as Dmitrei and Mr. Davis had. The rest were now stuck indoors, where they would eventually starve if they didn't find a way to get more food. And how long would the power stay on? How long would the plumbing keep working? There were probably some workers stuck at the power plant, so they could keep things running for a while. But if any power lines went down, they'd have a hard time sending crews out to fix them. Anyone who lost power would likely stay without it until the invasion was over.

If it ever ended. I suddenly remembered an old William Shatner movie about swarms of spiders. The characters managed to survive the night, but in the morning they found that the whole planet was covered in webbing. That final shot gave me nightmares.

Eventually I fell back asleep, but I probably woke up every hour.

A little before seven AM, Song started screaming. Greg burst into the room, hitting me in the head with the door. I sat up and got to my feet as quickly as I could. Greg held his bat over Song's head, ready to smash her brains in at the first sign of zombieism. I put my hand on his chest and pushed him back, then leaned over Song.

Her wounds had turned into gigantic boils, which seemed to undulate and quiver. She had one on each hand, three on her left arm, and two on her right. Song started to convulse. I had no idea what to do, so I just leaned over her and put a hand on her shoulder. One of the pustules popped open, and a zombie fairy climbed out.

I took a step back, stunned with fear. The fairy got to its feet, tested its wings, and took to the air. Greg nearly took my head off swinging his bat in the cramped little room. I ducked to the floor while he took a few more swings, smashing pictures on walls and severely denting a filing cabinet. He finally got it on his fourth swing, but more fairies started hatching.

I crawled out of the room so I wouldn't become another casualty. Then I stood outside the door, my bat at the ready, to take down any fairies that got past Greg. I'll spare you the details, but between the two of us, we managed to kill each of the hatching fairies. And when more hatched from Lea an hour later, we took care of those too.

Song started to feel better almost immediately after the hatching. We wrapped up her wounds with gauze, and her color returned to her face. Lea was a bit worse off, because in his enthusiasm, Greg had struck her arm to kill a hatching fairy. It wasn't broken, but it put her in tremendous pain. We worked together to put her arm in a sling.

We decided that with a few dixies – that's what I'm calling them, it's short for "dead pixie" – loose in the building, we'd spend most of our time in smaller rooms, and we'd go everywhere in pairs. Eira and I were in the cafeteria's kitchen, getting some lunch together for the group, when Eira suddenly stood perfectly still. It took me a minute to notice she was staring at me through those huge glasses she wears.

"What's wrong?" I asked.

"Don't… move… a muscle," she said quietly. She slowly reached to her left and grabbed a baking pan. I heard a buzzing just over the top of my head, and I had to force myself to stand still. Eira now held the pan in both hands and lifted it above her head. "Now, duck!" she yelled, and I dropped to the floor.

Eira rushed towards me, and I heard a loud "spang" sound as she swiped the pan through the air. Something hit the fridge door behind me, and I saw the dixie land on the floor, just a few feet away. It was stunned, and two of its wings were broken.

While I climbed to my feet, Eira rushed past me carrying a plastic storage container, about the size of a loaf of bread. She slammed it down over the dixie, trapping it inside. "Hand me that lid," she said, and I passed it over. She set the lid on the floor and carefully slid the container over it, then locked it in place. Then she stood, grabbed a knife off of a magnetic strip on the wall, and poked a few holes in the lid.

"What are you doing?" I asked.

"Science class!" she said, as if that explained everything. Eira doesn't usually talk much; she's always seemed kind of shy. And when she does get excited about something, the rest of us have trouble following her train of thought. But she's a straight-A student, so I generally assume she knows what she's talking about. She ran down the hallway, and I followed.

The science classroom had eight rectangular tables, each of which could seat four students. The room also featured a sink, some cabinets, and the teacher's desk. On the far side of the classroom was another door, which led to a storage closet. As I entered the room, Eira held the storage container under one arm and was trying to get into the closet.

"Locked," she said, turning towards me. "Can you help me get this open?"

"I think I saw some keys in the principal's office," I said, and went to go get them. I ran into Greg, Song, and Lea as I searched the office, and they were intrigued enough to follow me back to the science classroom. Song and Lea were feeling much better.

There were a lot of keys, and it took twelve tries before we found the right one. Eira handed the storage container to Greg. Then she started looking through all the different bottles and jugs of chemicals. She grabbed three jugs of liquid, handed them to us, then went back into the closet for more.

"What are these for?" Song asked, setting a jug down on the table.

"The fairies - they're from another dimension, right?" Eira asked. Song shrugged, but Eira just kept going. "So they're probably affected by different chemicals. A formula that's deadly to us might be harmless to them, and vice versa. We just have to test a few combinations on this fairy —"

"Dixie," I interrupted.

"That's not going to catch on," Song said.

"...and figure out what's deadly to them," Eira said. "If we're lucky, we'll find something that's not too dangerous to humans, and we can spray it around the building."

"Whatever you figure out, I doubt there's enough of it in this building to last us very long," Lea said.

"Still worth trying," Eira said.

"Just be careful," Song said. "It would suck to survive those dixie attacks and then get killed by homemade mustard gas."

"You said dixie," I said.

"Shut up," Song said, then pulled me in for a hug. I was glad she was feeling better.

We hung out in the science lab for a while, helping Eira try different combinations of chemicals on the dixie. We usually kept the doors closed in whatever room we were in, but with all the fumes in the air, we had to keep it open. We made sure at least one of us kept our eyes on the door at all times, in case of unwelcome visitors.

For a while, the four of us sat and talked while Eira worked behind us. It felt strangely normal, though the conversational topics weren't quite as upbeat as usual.

"I miss my dog," Lea said.

"Is he, uh... an indoor dog or an outdoor dog?" Greg asked.

Lea took a deep breath before answering. "A bit of both," she finally said. "But... mostly outdoor."

"Oh," Greg said, and changed the subject.

After about an hour, Song accompanied me to the cafeteria to finish getting lunch together, and we brought some hot dogs and fries back to the science lab. Eira was so into her work that it was hard to get her to eat.

The rest of us got bored after a while. Song and I stayed with Eira while Greg and Lea got some other things done around the building. Greg had some idea about determining the safest room in the building and making it more livable, so we'd have a good place to retreat if the dixies got in.

Honestly I think he just wanted to be alone with Lea. For the last few hours he'd been fawning over her more than the rest of us. Maybe he was afraid we were the last girls on

Earth, and Lea was the only one of us who wasn't gay or a nerd. But whatever it was, Lea didn't seem to mind.

I didn't mind either, as it meant more alone time with Song. Okay, so we weren't completely alone, but Eira so rarely looked up from her work that we might as well have been. Song and I sat and talked, and while it wasn't the most romantic of circumstances – especially with the shrill screams we occasionally heard from Eira's captive – it was still pretty nice.

The sun was setting when Eira suddenly shouted out, "Eureeka!" It kind of sounded rehearsed, like she'd wanted to shout that all her life. She called us over for a look. It was a combination of three chemicals. She said they were common chemicals, but I'd never heard of them, and each had at least six syllables. The combination became a liquid that dissolved the dixie's skin on contact, but it was harmless enough to use around humans.

"I mean, I wouldn't drink it," Eira said. "But the fumes are harmless. You're not going to hurt yourself if you spill some on your skin."

"Great," I said. "But what do we do with it? Find some water guns?"

"Think bigger," Eira said. "If I can get this information to the military, they can use it to save the world."

"Okay," Song said, pulling out her phone. "But we haven't had cell service since we got here."

Eira thought a moment and asked, "Anybody tried the landlines?"

I've never felt stupider in my life. In my defense, we'd been busy, in one life-or-death situation after another. None of us had been thinking clearly. Plus, I've only used a landline maybe three times in my life, so they don't even register as phones to me. Also, I hadn't heard them ring since we got there. Surely if they worked, they'd have been ringing off the hook. Besides, there were five of us, so I wasn't alone in my stupidity.

The three of us headed for the secretary's office and looked at the phone. The ringer was turned off, but there were fifty messages on the answering machine. I picked up the handset and put it to my ear. There was indeed a dial tone. "Who do we call?" Song asked, but I was already dialing my mom's number. I got a message saying the call couldn't go through.

"If you're dialing a cell phone, that's not going to work," Eira said. "You're only going to be able to reach other landlines."

Oh. Duh. But my house didn't have a landline. Then I tried 911 but got a busy signal.

"There's another phone in the principal's office," Eira said. "Both of you keep trying any emergency service you can reach. I'm going to see if I can find any other numbers to dial. Something that won't be so overloaded." While Song and I kept dialing, Eira started looking through the shelves in the secretary's office. She pulled out an old phonebook and thumbed through it. "Aha," she finally said.

"Found something?" I asked, hanging up the phone.

"Give me that," she said, bringing her book over. I stood aside and watched her dial. I looked at the page she was on, and it had something to do with the military.

Just then, Greg and Lea showed up. "Hey, what's going on?" Greg asked.

"We think we found—" I started to say, but then there was a noise from somewhere else in the building. A loud knocking sound.

"That sounded like the front door," Greg said.

We left Eira and Song with their phones, while Greg, Lea, and I went to check it out.

The building had two front doors, and the banging was coming from the farther of the two. We ran down the main hallway, then turned the corner. We could now see the doors at the end of the hallway, and my blood froze at what I saw. A man was trying to get into the building, but the doors were locked. Dixies were swarming all over him, and he kept knocking them away with a crowbar.

Whenever he had a chance, he tried prying the door open with the crowbar. When that didn't work, he started banging on the glass.

"No! Don't!" Greg yelled, running down the hallway toward the front door. Lea and I just stood frozen in place. Greg reached the front door right as the glass shattered. He skidded to a halt and turned around. Behind him, the visitor tried climbing through the hole he'd made, but he was overwhelmed by the swarm. Then dixies started flowing in through the shattered window.

My first thought was to get back to the office so I could be with Song. But with a thousand dixies nipping at my heels, I couldn't be that picky. I ran through the first door I saw and slammed the door behind me. I jumped when I saw that Lea had made it in with me. There was a narrow, vertical window on the door, and I looked through it. The hallway was a thick cloud of dixies, but I could still make out the scene at the end of the hall. Greg had been skeletonized, as had the man who'd broken the window.

"Greg?" Lea asked. I shook my head, and she buried her face in her hands.

I turned, put my back against the door, and slowly sat down. Lea sat down beside me. Neither of us spoke. I looked around the room. We were in the band room. I thought about Song and Eira. Had they managed to get the office door closed in time? Or were they so busy with the phones that they didn't know there was a problem until it was too late? Would I ever find out?

The band room was one of the biggest rooms in the building, but it didn't have any food or water. If this was our last refuge, our days were numbered. I stood up and grabbed a chair, wedging it under the door handle. As far as I knew the dixies couldn't open doors, but why take the chance?

I looked out into the hallway again. There really was no way out. I wanted to get to the office and see if Song was okay. But I knew I'd be dead before I got halfway there. I hoped Song didn't try to come save me. I realized Lea was sobbing, and I sat down again to comfort her. The problem was, I couldn't think of any words, as I felt every bit as desperate as she did.

"I always thought the glass was shatterproof," Lea said, her voice devoid of emotion. I didn't reply.

There was another window on the opposite wall, next to an emergency exit. Through that window, I could see the air was thick with the creatures. Just like the air in the hallway. I stood up and walked over to the window, looking out at the world. The school was on a bit of a hill, and through the swarm, I could see a quiet neighborhood below. A couple of wrecked cars sat on the sidewalk, but other than that it looked picturesque.

I looked at the emergency exit. I wondered what would happen if I ran out the door. Could I make it to one of those houses, or would I be eaten before I got halfway? At least I'd die quickly, rather than dying of thirst and hunger. I shook my head, crossed the room again, and sat next to Lea for the third time.

It was too early to be thinking about ending things that way. I could still taste the last meal I'd eaten, and I was already worrying about starvation? Screw that. There was still time for a miracle. Running out the door was always an option if things got hopeless. I found that thought oddly comforting. But I wasn't going to jump the gun.

I don't know how many hours Lea and I sat there, staring off into space, but suddenly it was morning. Lea's head was in my lap and I really had to pee. I gently moved her head, trying not to wake her up. She murmured something about her dog but kept snoring. I stood up, looking for a place to pee that wouldn't smell too bad. There was an alcove on one wall where the band students hung their uniforms. I didn't see any better prospects, so I started making my way across the room.

Then I heard a roar – not like a lion, but like a racecar. There was movement outside the window, beyond the normal movement of the swarm. Though my bladder was still screaming at me, I ran to the window and looked outside.

Military jets were everywhere, flying back and forth across the sky. Some of them started spraying a blue mist down below, like they were cropdusters. The mist was soon everywhere, like a blue fog had rolled in. And then it started raining dixies. They fell out of the sky by the thousands. A couple of the dixies close to the window started choking, then their skin just started melting away like one of those effervescent tablets you put in water when you have a stomachache.

The fog started creeping in under the exit door. I could now smell it. It smelled exactly like the concoction Eira had put together in the lab. Was this her doing? Had she gotten through to the military?

I ran to the other door and looked into the school hallway. The blue mist was already making its way through the halls. Everywhere I looked, dixies were dying. Their wings went first, sending them crashing to the ground, and then their skin melted away. It was both disgusting and beautiful.

When I felt it was safe, I opened the door. Lea woke up at this and grabbed my ankle. "What are you doing?"

"It's okay, Lea," I said. "I think it's finally safe."

As I poked my head into the hallway, I heard another door open farther down the hall. Song and Eira stepped out of the office, their eyes full of amazement.

"Song!" I shouted, and we ran to each other, tiny skeletons crunching beneath our feet. We collided into a tight hug.

"Rahima," she said. "I… I… really need to pee."

"Me too," I said, laughing. The four of us ran to the girls' room, happy that the nightmare was over.

Oh, and I'm also pleased to report that Lea's dog was okay.

Telethon

"Citizens of Gantua City, it is I, Sonikron, master of sound and super genius extraordinaire. Today, I have done what no other supervillain could accomplish. Using my vast intellect, I have captured your most beloved hero, Rainbow Man."

The villain made a sweeping gesture to his left, and the camera zoomed out, revealing the sight of Rainbow Man hanging from a set of manacles. He wore his usual brightly-colored tights and a mask that obscured the upper half of his face. He appeared to be conscious, but he looked tired and weak.

"So what happens next? Am I going to kill him? Torture him? Unmask him? Well, my friends, that all depends on you! This town is full of supervillains, many of whom have personal grudges against my odious prisoner. So it is for you and only you, my fellow miscreants, that I'm proud to announce this once-in-a-lifetime event. That's right, Rainbow Man's fate will be determined by a telethon!"

A website URL began flashing at the bottom of the screen. "Simply visit my website, where you can make anonymous, untraceable donations. When we reach one thousand dollars, I'll punch him in the stomach. When we reach two thousand dollars, I'll punch him in the face. When I reach three thousand dollars..."

Dizzy and barely conscious, Rainbow Man half-listened to Sonikron's announcement. He knew the broadcast was going out to the entire city, maybe even the entire state. With the number of villains running rampant in Gantua City, Rainbow Man knew that the money would be pouring in. He zoned in and out, looking for any way to escape. His powers weren't working, and he couldn't focus enough to figure out why.

"...I'll break his kneecaps with a baseball bat. At one hundred thousand dollars, I'll hold a match to his groin. When we reach five hundred thousand dollars..."

There was a monitor to the left of the camera, showing the donations coming in. Barely five minutes into the broadcast, it had already reached seven hundred dollars. Soon the word would reach the rest of the villains in town. When the criminal masterminds started turning on their televisions, the donations would skyrocket.

"At a million, things start to get interesting," Sonikron said. "That's when I'll remove his mask, and reveal his identity to the world. But the fun won't end there. If the total gets up to five million, I'll..."

Where even am I? Rainbow Man thought. He looked around for clues. They were in a rectangular room, maybe twelve by fifteen feet. It had an unused look about it, like it had been empty for years before Sonikron moved his equipment in. There was one door and one window. Unpainted walls, office-style ceiling, tile floor, no carpet. No real furniture, just wooden crates and cardboard boxes. Sonikron's equipment sat on one crate.

There was another crate to his right, on which sat what looked like an old radio. Except it wasn't a radio, it was a custom-made transmitter of some sort. Rainbow Man tried to think. He'd seen a similar device recently... yes, Sonikron had been wearing a smaller version on his wrist during their fight earlier.

That had to be what was suppressing his powers.

Rainbow Man's abilities were psychic-based, and the right subsonic frequency could mess with his brain enough to keep his powers from working. He had to find a way to shut off that radio. If there were just some way he could reach it. It was only about five feet away, but it might as well have been a mile. Rainbow Man's hands were tightly manacled, and he couldn't even begin to summon his powers.

"...guaranteeing that he'll never have children. And finally, if the fund reaches a grand total of one hundred million dollars, I will snuff out this poor hero's life. Think about that. Never again will you have to worry about your plans being foiled. Never again will you hear that insipid catchphrase of his. Never again will you find yourself wrapped in those silly rainbow beams. Never again will..."

He just had to concentrate. Surely there was some way to close his mind off from the brain-numbing frequency. He just needed his powers for a second. A single chromatic blast would be enough to smash the radio and get himself free.

But try as he might, he couldn't get through the mental block. Freedom was just a few feet away, just out that window...

The window. He couldn't see much, but he didn't have to. He recognized the building across the street. He spent so much time flying around Gantua City that he could do it with his eyes closed. They had to be in the abandoned office building across the street from First Gantua Bank. All he had to do was...

"Never again," Sonikron said. "So reach deep into your pockets, friends. Give until it hurts. It will be worth it to all of you in the long... eh?" On the monitor, he saw Rainbow Man mouthing something behind him. "A moment," he said, and turned toward his enemy.

"That just won't do," Sonikron said. He grabbed a roll of duct tape off the top of a crate, ripped off a piece, and slapped it over Rainbow Man's mouth. Then, just for fun, he punched Rainbow Man in the gut.

"My apologies," the villain said, turning back to the cameras. "Sometimes he thinks he's clever. As I was saying..."

Rainbow Man was seeing stars. Without his rainbow shields, pain felt so much stronger. Sonikron wasn't a heavy hitter, but Rainbow Man had become so used to feeling invincible that even weak punches felt like being kicked by a donkey. *I've let myself get soft*, Rainbow Man thought, but he couldn't dwell on that now. He had to hang onto what faculties he had left and devise a way to escape.

His time was short. His mind and body were both in a weakened state. He had no powers. He had no weapons. He had no way of escape. But he did have one thing Sonikron didn't know about.

He had a boyfriend.

Just a few blocks away, Ronnie Robertson watched the broadcast in horror. He was the only person in Gantua City who knew that mild-mannered limo driver Rayne Bowman was actually the superhero Rainbow Man. Now he watched his lover hang limply in the background while a psychotic villain asked people to pledge money to his insane cause.

And finally, if the fun reaches a grant total of one hundred melon dollars I will snuff out this poor heros life. The words appeared at the bottom of the screen, the live captioning system spelling most of the words correctly for a change. Ronnie felt numb, every bit as helpless as his dear, sweet Rayne. He had to do something, but what? He didn't even know where Rayne was being held. And even if he did, Ronnie didn't have any powers. If this "Sonikron" was powerful enough to take down a superhero, what chance did a mere mortal have? He didn't even own a gun.

Ronnie was no weakling. He'd even beaten Rayne at arm wrestling on more than one occasion. But "guy who goes to the gym" versus "high-tech supervillain" wasn't much of a matchup. And then there was Ronnie's deafness. If he ran to Rayne's rescue, he'd have no way of knowing if he was making too much noise, so he couldn't be sure he was being stealthy. Nor would he be able to hear it if Sonikron approached from behind. He'd be dead before he even knew he'd been discovered.

On the television, Rayne was starting to mouth something. Three... one... seven... And then Sonikron saw what he was up to, and covered Rayne's mouth with duct tape. Ronnie picked up his phone and started typing "317" into the maps app. Hundreds of results came up in Gantua city alone. And he didn't even know if that was the full number.

The ticker at the bottom of the screen showed that the pledge level was now up to two thousand dollars. To reward those pledging, Sonikron turned and punched Rayne in the face. Ronnie winced, tears starting to well in his eyes. Blood dribbled down from Rayne's nose, and Ronnie started to avert his eyes...

But then he noticed something. Rayne was moving his fingers in a very specific way. To the untrained eye, it looked like idle movements, maybe even spasms from the pain. But Ronnie recognized it as a tactile sign language. Ronnie had taught it to Rayne so they could still speak to each other when the lights were off. Rayne was now touching his own palms using the code Ronnie knew so well.

Three... One... Seven... Five... South... Green... Street. He kept tapping out the same message over and over. Ronnie knew that street. It wasn't far. He thought about notifying the police. He couldn't speak, but the police had a text line for those who couldn't use the main number. Unfortunately, Ronnie had texted them before and hadn't been impressed with the speed of their response. The police were most likely overwhelmed with well-meaning tipsters right now, and it would be forever before they had time to look into each tip. Ronnie sent them a text anyway, but he knew he had to do more.

This is stupid, he thought, as he grabbed a couple of things and headed out the door.

The office building had never been used. It had been built two years earlier, but the company had gone out of business before moving in, and no one else had bought it yet. The back door was unlocked, or rather, the lock had been broken. Ronnie entered the lobby, wondering if he'd already been spotted. The building was six stories tall, and he knew that if he took the time to check every room on every floor, Rayne would be long gone by the time Ronnie found him.

The lights were on in the lobby. This struck Ronnie as strange since the building wasn't officially in use. Who pays the electric bill when the company goes out of business? It didn't matter, and he was getting distracted. But the lights gave him an idea. The fuse box. If he could figure out how to cut power to the building, that would at least end the telethon, buying him some time. Well, maybe. It depended on what sort of equipment Sonikron was using. At any rate, it was worth a try.

He searched around the first floor but found only empty offices. He wondered if the building had a basement. He decided against taking the elevator, as he wasn't sure if it made noise. He found a stairwell and took it to the basement. The lowest floor was mostly utility and storage rooms. On the wall opposite the elevator, Ronnie spotted a panel on the wall marked "Electrical," and made a beeline for it.

The panel was locked with a padlock, but he'd been prepared for that. He didn't own a gun, but he hadn't wanted to come completely unarmed, so he'd brought a hammer. Hoping Sonikron wasn't within earshot, Ronnie started hammering on the padlock.

He didn't hear the "ding" as the elevator doors opened behind him. He didn't hear Sonikron shout at him. As he repeatedly struck the lock, he noticed a shadow fall across the wall, and he turned around. Sonikron had his gun raised and was shouting something Ronnie couldn't decipher. Before Ronnie could even react, Sonikron fired.

Nothing happened. The villain looked confused, then fired again, squeezing the trigger over and over. Dropping the gun, he pulled another device out of his pocket, a small white box with a button on it. He pressed the button, then looked surprised when Ronnie didn't react.

And then Ronnie understood. All of Sonikron's weapons – every last one of them – were sound-based. His whole shtick was to incapacitate people with headache-inducing sound waves. It had worked so well for him in the past, that it never even occurred to him to bring backup weapons. But Ronnie was immune to such devices.

Sonikron frantically searched through his pockets for more weapons, but he hadn't brought anything that was a match for Ronnie's hammer. Realizing he was no longer in control of the situation, Sonikron turned and ran.

Three... One... Seven... Five... South... Green... Street. Three... One... Seven... Five... South... Green... Street. Three... One... Seven... Five... South... Green... Street.

Rainbow Man kept tapping the letters and numbers out on his palm, over and over, hoping someone would get the message before Sonikron came back. Even with the villain gone, the pledge totals on the screen kept rising, and Rainbow Man was in for a world of hurt when his captor returned.

The door opened, but it wasn't Sonikron who entered. *Ronnie?* Rainbow Man thought, not believing his eyes.

Ronnie unplugged the camera and threw it on the floor. Then he searched the room until he found the keys to the manacles. The restraints came undone, and Rayne ripped off the duct tape and fell into Ronnie's arms. "My hero," Rayne said, as Ronnie helped him to the floor. Rayne pointed to the sonic device that was blocking his powers, and Ronnie smashed it with his blood-covered hammer.

Sonikron did not recover from his injuries. A lawsuit against Ronnie would be forthcoming, but the mayor of Gantua City promised that the city would pay for his legal defense.

In recognition of his act of heroism, Ronnie was offered the key to the city. He politely declined the award. He didn't feel like a hero. His motivations had been more selfish than anything, as far as he was concerned. He hadn't set out to rescue a superhero or to bring down a dangerous villain. His only goal had been to save the man he loved so that they could go on enjoying each other's company for years to come.

And no reward could ever top that.

Social Cues

"Why are you so weird?" Toby asked.

The question came out of the blue, and Zyna had no idea what he was talking about. She looked up and down, doing a quick mental checklist of social protocols. She couldn't think of a single weird thing she'd done in the last five minutes. She'd barely even spoken since they'd started eating. "Can you be more specific?" she finally asked.

"First, you ate all your fries before you even unwrapped your burger," Toby began.

"They get cold the fastest," Zyna replied.

"Then you ate all the tomatoes off your burger," Toby said. "Then the pickles. Then the bun. Now you're eating the meat by itself."

Zyna set down the cheese-covered burger patty. "That's weird?" she asked.

"Do you see anybody else doing it?" Toby asked.

Zyna looked around the fast food restaurant. She didn't see anyone eating their burgers one piece at a time, but she still didn't get why that would make it weird. "It's just how I've always done it," she said. She could have gone into greater detail, but she didn't. She could have told him that she ate the ingredients in that order because that was the order in which she liked the ingredients. She could have told him that she ate the meat last because the final bite sticks around in your mouth the longest. Eat the worst first, save the best for last. She'd done it that way for so long that she no longer even thought about it.

Toby shrugged. "It's okay, I like weird," he said.

"Cool," Zyna said, forcing herself to smile. She'd always worn her individuality on her sleeve, but in truth, it was a defense mechanism. People always noticed your quirks eventually, so it was better to just show them off and pretend you were proud of them. And to some extent, she was. But part of her also longed to blend into the crowd.

It all came down to which quirks were planned. If people called her weird because she dyed her hair purple or wore a strange outfit, she could prepare for their reactions, and she enjoyed the attention. But when people randomly pointed out things she did that she'd never thought of as abnormal, she felt like she'd failed as a human being.

She'd once told her mom how different she felt. Her mother had told her, "Don't worry. Everyone feels that way." But Zyna wasn't so sure. Growing up, some of her classmates showed such ease when it came to social interaction. But Zyna had always felt like an observer, like some extra-terrestrial, sent to Earth to study the humans and learn their mysterious ways.

Now that she was in college, things were a little better. The students at the university were so much more diverse than Zyna's high school classmates had been. She still felt like a misfit, but she was among other misfits, so she didn't stand out. Unfortunately, this more comfortable environment meant she was more likely to let her guard down. When she did stand out, she felt all the more called out. It was one thing to be called strange by normies, but being called weird by a fellow outcast was another level entirely.

It hurt, but she didn't intend to change. She liked the way she ate, and if it cost her a friend or two, then they weren't really friends in the first place.

"So what do you think?" Toby asked.

Zyna blinked. She'd been so lost in thought that she'd missed the question. She cocked her head like a puppy. "Huh?" she asked.

Toby chuckled in a way that said, *Typical Zyna*. He made sure she was looking into his eyes and asked, "Movie at my place? My parents aren't home, so we'll have the whole place to ourselves."

"Sure," Zyna said, looking forward to some time away from the noisy dorms.

Toby lived a few blocks from the university. He also had a dorm room, as school policy prohibited living off-campus, but he didn't spend much time there.

It was the first time Zyna had seen his house. As they got out of Toby's car, Zyna stared at the old home with her mouth open. It was three stories tall, though she wouldn't have called it a mansion. It looked more than a century old, but its antiquated style fit right in with the rest of the houses on the street. The house was taller than it was wide and had very little yard. The paint was peeling in spots, and one of the shutters was off its hinge, but to Zyna, it was a dream home.

"You really live here?" she asked.

"Would I take you to someone else's house?" Toby asked back.

"Smart ass," Zyna replied. He was always doing that, answering a question with a question, making her feel stupid for asking.

She followed him inside and he showed her around. The house had a lot of old-school charm, with plenty of antique furniture to match the structure. Zyna was afraid to touch anything, despite Toby's assurances that it was fine. Everything about the place felt really "thin" to Zyna, but she couldn't put the concept into words. The staircases seemed narrow and steep compared to modern houses, the walls weren't very thick, and the high ceilings somehow added to the skinny theme. It was like they'd taken a much wider house and squinched it.

Toby invited her to sit on the sofa in the living room. The couch was red with a paisley design, and it creaked a little when she sat down. A modern high-definition television hung across from her above the fireplace, somewhat ruining the home's theme.

"Can I get you a drink?" Toby asked, and Zyna nodded. He disappeared into the kitchen for a minute and came back with two glasses filled with cola. He handed one to Zyna.

She took a sip, then got a strange look on her face. "What's in this?" she asked.

"Just a little rum," Toby said. "To take the edge off."

"I'm only twenty," Zyna said. She looked for a place to set the glass down but didn't want to leave a ring on the antique end table.

"I won't tell anyone," Toby said. He saw her predicament and placed a coaster on the end table. Then he sat down next to her.

Zyna set the glass down. She was mildly annoyed that he hadn't asked her if she wanted a drink, but then she realized he actually had. Had she missed a social cue? It wouldn't be the first time in her life. Heck, it wouldn't be the first time in the last hour. She decided to let it go. She'd make a point of sipping her drink extra slowly.

Toby loaded up a movie. It was one of Zyna's favorites. She remembered telling him how much she loved the movie, and while she appreciated that he'd remembered, she thought it was a little odd that he'd invited her over to watch a movie she'd already seen multiple times. *Let it go,* she reminded herself once again. *He's probably just being nice.*

Approximately ten minutes into the movie, Toby put his arm around her shoulder. Zyna froze, her mind racing. She only thought of Toby as a friend, and she'd thought he felt the same way. Had she been missing signals all this time?

But that didn't make any sense. Toby was one of the few students on campus who knew she was transgender. In fact, part of the reason she'd told him she was trans was to ensure he wasn't just trying to get into her pants.

Somewhere between confused and terrified, she turned her head and gave him a strange look. He turned to her, leaned in, and kissed her hard on the lips.

"Whoa whoa whoa," Zyna said, backing away from him.

"What's the problem?" Toby asked. "You like me, right?"

"Not *that* way," Zyna said. "What are you doing?"

"We're just friends having fun," Toby said. He leaned forward again, putting his hands on her shoulders.

"I don't have what you're looking for," Zyna said.

"We can stay above the waistline," Toby said. "At least, *I* can." He kept glancing from her mouth to his own crotch, and it took a few seconds for Zyna to understand what he meant.

"Why did you think I'd want to do *that?*" she asked.

"You seemed up for it when I asked you here," he said.

Zyna had no idea what he meant. She stared at him for a few seconds and finally said, "You said movie..."

"I said my parents weren't home," Toby clarified.

Ooooh, Zyna thought. Once again she'd failed to read between the lines. Why did people have to say everything in code? "I didn't mean to lead you on," she heard herself say. *Why am I apologizing?* she thought. *He damn near sexually assaulted me.*

"No harm done," Toby said. "If you're really not interested, that's your loss. I'm between girlfriends right now, and thought I could get a little FWB action. But if it's not your thing, it's all good."

It sounded reasonable to Zyna. Sort of. "Thank you," she said, starting to calm down.

"Don't worry about me," Toby said. "I can hold out for a real girl."

Zyna heard an odd little squeak escape her lips. She stood

up, reached for her drink, and threw it in his face. Then she carefully set the empty glass back down on the coaster and walked out Toby's front door. He didn't follow.

As she walked, she thought about everything he'd ever said to her, looking for missed cues. Then she thought about damage control. He'd be mad at her, would he start telling everyone she was trans? For half a second, she thought about going back to apologize. *Screw that*, she thought.

For years she'd suspected that she might be neurodivergent, but she'd never bothered to find out for sure. She wasn't sure she ever wanted to know. It was like a box that couldn't be closed once opened. She was afraid the knowledge would change her forever. She didn't want to self-diagnose, but she followed a large number of autistic people on social media, and she'd always found their posts relatable. She wondered if that was why she had so much trouble communicating with people.

Still, even for a miscommunication, Toby had gone over the line. Zyna wasn't into guys, or girls for that matter, and she thought Toby knew that. She was sure she'd mentioned it early on in their friendship. And later, when she'd told him she was trans, Toby had made it clear he was only interested in dating cis women. She'd wondered at the time if his attitude was transphobic, but since she wasn't interested in dating him anyway, she'd let it slide.

But now that she thought about it, she'd let a lot of things slide. Hindsight showed her a plethora of red flags, none of which had seemed so bad when taken one at a time. She'd grown up without a lot of friends, and her enthusiasm for acceptance had caused her to ignore a lot of Toby's bad behavior.

Unfortunately, that meant she was friendless again. She'd have to look at her other acquaintances and see if any of them seemed upgradable to friendship status. *Upgradable to friendship status?* she thought. *This is why people don't talk to you.*

She was halfway back to campus now, but she wasn't

walking quite as fast. She'd been furious when she'd started, her feet pounding the sidewalk like an angry marching band. But now she was starting to enjoy being out. Winter was almost over, and the air was just the right temperature for a nice walk. She'd never been in this neighborhood before, and it was fun looking at all the old houses.

A shadow crossed over her, and at first she thought it was a cloud passing over the sun. But then she felt a weird tug at her clothing. There was a weightless feeling in her stomach, and her hair stood on end. A blue light surrounded her. She looked up and saw a giant floating disc overhead. Then her feet left the ground, and she felt herself being pulled toward the flying saucer.

Here we go again, she thought. She hoped it would at least be the grays this time.

Six years earlier, the saucers started showing up. At first, people thought it was a hoax. Some countries almost went to war, suspecting the ships were spy drones or bombers sent by their enemies. Some governments fired at the saucers, but quickly realized their weapons were ineffective. Any missiles that approached the ships were harmlessly teleported away. The saucers never retaliated, but just hovered there. Panic spread across the globe.

Then they started abducting people. Those who were taken aboard the ships were returned unharmed. The aliens were reportedly friendly and curious, and just wanted to know more about our world. They had no use for Earth's resources and simply saw the planet as sort of a zoo. They watched humans the same way humans went on safaris to take pictures of tigers. Sometimes they'd pull humans on board their ships to study them more closely, but they never tried to hurt them.

Some people still didn't trust the aliens, but there wasn't much they could do about it. The global panic gradually abated, as humans had more things to worry about. Now, six years later, the discs were just another feature in the sky, and getting abducted was considered a mild inconvenience.

Roughly a tenth of the planet's population had been taken at one point or another. The earliest abductees had become famous, and many had gone on to write best-selling novels about their experiences. But those stories were so common now, that people had lost interest. At best it could be used as an excuse for being late to work. Sometimes the aliens would even write them a note.

Zyna sat on a padded examination chair. She'd already taken off her shoes; she knew the routine. This was her sixth time getting abducted – twice by the lizard people, four times by the grays. She preferred the grays. They were generally better at speaking English, and seemed to have more empathy. Also, their ships smelled better. *Is that racist?* Zyna wondered.

A metal orb floated into the room and scanned her with a beam of yellow light. Digital readouts on the wall started filling with what Zyna assumed were her vital statistics. One wall of the examination room was transparent, and a pair of gray-skinned aliens stood on the other side, talking to each other. They were bald with large black eyes, and they wore loose-fitting jumpsuits.

"It is well to see you again," said one of the grays. His voice was transmitted into the examination room through a speaker. The gray couldn't enter the room itself due to having different environmental needs.

"Hi, Gorb," Zyna said, recognizing him by his deep voice. "What brings me here?"

"It is being the usual," Gorb said in his stilted accent. "We are the being here to learn more about you."

"Why me, though?" Zyna asked. "Most people haven't even been picked once."

"I am apologies," Gorb said. "It is the being better to leave the most population undertouched, so the observation is not to change the results of data. It is also that by taking the same people again, we can monitor to their age and other progress."

Zyna thought she understood, but it didn't make it any less intrusive. At least she didn't have any more classes that day.

"And also besides," Gorb added, "I am enjoy to see you again. Yours is one of my favorite humans."

"Thanks, I guess," Zyna said. This was the third time she'd been examined by Gorb, and she'd developed more of a rapport with him than any of the other aliens. Still, she wasn't sure what Gorb saw in her. "But what do you possibly get out of studying me?" she asked. "I'm not typical. I'm about as different as you can get. If you're trying to learn about humans, I am not a good example of the average human being. I've been told I'm weird."

Gorb made a sneezing sound, which Zyna understood to be laughter. She still didn't understand their sense of humor. Their laugh-sneeze reaction seemed to have as much to do with compassion as it did absurdity. In this case the noise meant, "Don't be silly, you're valid."

"I'm serious," Zyna said. "I can't even have a normal conversation with other human beings."

"You are being understand us more than most of yours," Gorb said.

"That's because you say what you mean," Zyna said. "You might use the wrong words, but at least you're straightforward."

"Then it is not humans you are being wrong talk to," Gorb said. "It is liars."

"They're not really liars," Zyna said. "They're just so used to speaking in metaphors, they don't even know they're doing it. And they expect others to understand them. And for the most part, the others do. I'm the outlier."

"Zyna, please to listen," Gorb said. His face took on a wide-eyed expression that would have horrified most humans, but Zyna understood it to be a look of sympathy.

"We have many scan of brains, yours and others of human. You are being correct. Yours is a difference."

"I knew it," Zyna said. She didn't know whether to be happy or sad. She'd always wanted the confirmation, but it still wasn't great news.

"Zyna," Gorb said again. "We are also having the technology to make it not different."

Zyna's eyes widened. "What?" she asked.

"If you could being more similar to the others human, would you?"

She didn't answer right away. She started thinking of all the times she'd been misunderstood, all the times she'd gotten the wrong impression, all the times she'd been called rude. She thought of the friendships she'd lost and the teachers who'd accused her of talking back. She'd been called antisocial for leaving a loud party, and she'd been called boring for refusing to try certain foods. Most recently she'd been called weird for the heinous act of eating a cheeseburger wrong.

Finally Zyna shook her head. "It's tempting," she said. "But no. This is who I am, and that big a change would be too much like killing the real me."

Gorb looked relieved. "Your choice is glad to me," he said. "But what on your other problem?"

"Other problem?" Zyna asked, but then she understood. "Oh, that." On her earlier visits, she'd discussed her gender dysphoria. The grays didn't seem to have much of a concept of gender, and Gorb had been fascinated by the concept. "Yes, I'd change my body if I could. I think about it every day."

Gorb's partner said something to him in their alien language. Gorb said something back, and the partner left the room. Turning back to Zyna, Gorb said, "But to another subject, we are in a problem, and you can being help us."

"What?" Zyna asked, her head cocked. These beings had godlike technology, what could they possibly need from her?

"The problem is in the Rez," Gorb said. From her previous visits, Zyna knew that Rez was their name for the lizard-like aliens who shared the skies with the grays. "When we were first arriving, the Shova and the Rez were in agree that we were only watch and learn the humans. But the Rez are now want to conquer. We the Shova are now protect humans."

It took a minute for the words to sink in, but once Zyna processed it, she was horrified. "The Rez want to invade Earth?" she asked.

"That is being it," Gorb said. "But don't to worry. We the Shova are more than the Rez. Ten for every one. If there is being fight, they are the lose."

"So what do you need me for?" Zyna asked.

"The leader of Shova is peace, and Rez is know Shova is not fight wanting. Leader is liking humans for watch, but not think is worth of protect."

That one took a minute to interpret. "Oh," Zyna said. "He thinks Earth is fun to watch, like a zoo. But not so much that he'd go to war for us. And the Rez know that about him."

"A sad yes," Gorb said. "But if you were in talk with leader…"

"You want *me* to represent Earth?" Zyna asked, incredulous. "Me? *I'm* supposed to convince him that Earth is worth saving?"

"There is the idea," Gorb said.

"Of all the people, why me?" Zyna asked.

"Because," Gorb said, "Of all people, you were the convince of me." He held his palm to his forehead, which seemed to be their equivalent of a human putting their hand over their heart.

A few hours later, Zyna met with the gray leader. His English wasn't quite as good as Gorb's, but he was a fast learner. Sitting face-to-face on opposite sides of a transparent metal wall, the two spoke for hours. Zyna didn't have to make an impassioned speech or an organized presentation. The two just had to get to know each other, so that the leader would see her as a person instead of a zoo animal.

She told him all about her life, her problems, and the little victories that kept her going. He told her many things she didn't know about Shova culture and anatomy. It occurred to Zyna that she now knew more about the Shova than anyone else on Earth, and she couldn't wait to tell someone about the experience. She just wasn't sure who.

When the meeting finally came to an end, the Shova leader assured her that Earth would be protected. Then she was returned to the examination room to say goodbye to Gorb.

Zyna woke up in what looked like a miniature hospital room. A woman in a green smock stood by her bed. "What happened?" Zyna asked. All the dreams of aliens and flying saucers were fading from her mind.

"You were hit by a car, dear," the doctor said. "You're in the campus infirmary. Don't worry, there's not a mark on you. Miracle, really."

Zyna didn't remember a car. The last thing she remembered was the walk home from Toby's. But she felt like she'd forgotten something big. She felt this odd sense of accomplishment, like she'd saved the world or something. She couldn't remember anything she'd done to warrant such a feeling. Maybe it was just the fact that she'd realized what a jerk Toby was, and had cut him out of her life. Whatever it was, she felt ready to take on the world.

The Rez took the Shova's threat seriously and left Earth to seek other planets. The Shova weren't far behind them. Without the threat of the Rez, the Shova didn't need to watch humans so closely. A few Shova ships remained nearby in case the Rez weren't true to their word, but they stayed far enough away that Earth wouldn't be able to detect them.

Before leaving, they wiped the humans' memory of their existence. It really wasn't that difficult. They'd already spent years planting subliminal post-hypnotic suggestions into Earth's media, preparing for their eventual departure. All they had to do now was to activate the signal, and most of the humans forgot they'd ever been there. After all, it was dangerous to leave primitive cultures with proof of extraterrestrial life.

Of course, there would be some physical evidence left behind, such as the books some of the abductees had written. But those would now be met with doubt, and as the years went on, they would fade into obscurity.

Gorb would miss Zyna, though. She was truly unique among her people. Against orders, he'd left her with one final gift. She'd wake up in the body she'd always wanted, with no memory of it ever having been otherwise. It was the least he could do.

Ray's Personal Blog

Saturday, January 1 3:16 PM

Hi, I'm Ray, short for Raymond. New year, new blog. I've decided I'm going to write more this year. I'm not really sure what I'm going to put on here. Probably just organize my thoughts and post when something interesting happens in my life, which is almost never.

Thursday, January 6 7:27 AM

I had a weird dream last night. I was in a car, and this cute guy I work with was driving us to the office. Except the road was a giant tongue, and he kept losing control because it was so slick. I could see the tongue's owner in the rearview mirror, a giant mouth that kept pace with us regardless of how fast we drove. I don't know what it meant but I woke up with an erection.

Note to self: Don't tell mom about this blog.

Friday, February 4 7:02 AM

Caught a great movie on streaming last night. "Slasher Party 7." Probably the best one of the series. The acting was so terrible, I couldn't stop laughing. It was made back in the day when movie blood was bright red, and nobody really cared about realism. This is why classic schlock horror will always be better than the torture porn they're making today.

Seriously, do modern filmmakers think we watch horror because we want to see realistic depictions of murder? Why would that be fun? If you want to see lifelike blood and guts, go to medical school. I, for one, just want to laugh in the face of death. The best horror doubles as comedy.

Saturday, July 23 10:48 AM

I forgot this thing was still here. Boy, that New Year's resolution didn't last long. I'll post a real blog soon, I promise.

Sunday, October 16 2:33 PM

For Halloween this year I'm turning my place into a mini haunted house for trick-or-treaters. I'm making a path that goes from the front door, through my living room, then the kitchen, and out the back door. I'm running a couple of ropes on each side of the path, and there will be lots of horror props along the sides. I've got blacklights, spiderwebs, motion-activated props, and all sorts of scary stuff. I'll guide each group through the house, and give them candy on their way out the back door. I've done it once before, and neighborhood kids really enjoyed it.

I swear this is one of the last neighborhoods in the world that celebrates Halloween properly. My friends tell me that they're lucky to see three groups of kids all night. These groups are usually driven by parents who go to multiple streets, looking for the rare house that has its porch light on. But on my street, at least half the houses are giving out candy, and parents feel safe enough to let their kids go out alone.

Unfortunately, we do get our share of teenage hooligans. Look, I'm not one of those guys who complains about plain-dressed teenagers showing up on Halloween. They're not my favorite kind of trick-or-treaters, but I'd rather they do that than go around egging houses. But some of these teens are just plain rude. They don't even say "trick-or-treat" anymore, they just hold out their pillowcases and expect free candy.

To me, Halloween is a barter system. You entertain me by showing up in a cool costume, and I reward you with candy. I realize some kids can't afford costumes, or don't have time to get one together, and I don't hold that against them. But some of these teens just seem so entitled. I don't know, maybe I'm just getting old. Why else would I start using words like "hooligans?"

Since Halloween's on a Monday, there was some discussion about whether our neighborhood would do candy on the 30th or 31st. But it looks like everyone's agreed to do it on Sunday the 30th.

Sunday, October 23 6:51 PM

Today I went to my Mom's to pick up some old Halloween decorations. When I was a kid, we had a life-sized grim reaper that will look great in my house. Mom gave me all the decorations she could find. While she was in the attic, she also found a box of my old comic books, so I took that too.

Tuesday, October 25 6:29 AM

When I got home from work last night, I started looking through my old comics. I flipped through a couple of superhero mags, and then I came to one of my old favorites: Sergeant Napalm's Warzone. These action-packed army stories were full of hot muscular men, often wrestling each other in ripped shirts. I think it may have been partly responsible for my gay awakening.

I got through the first 15 issues before I went to bed. I kept getting distracted because I thought I heard a rat scurrying in the walls. I'll have to think about hiring an exterminator. Maybe after Halloween. I don't want the exterminator thinking I'm some sort of freak when he sees all these horror props.

Tuesday, October 25 10:42 PM

My throat was a bit raspy today. I hope I don't get sick right before Halloween, that would suck. I keep a bag of cough drops in my desk at work. This brand prints inspiring messages on the wrappers, like "You can do this" and "The world is yours." But this one's messages said, "Prepare for his arrival," and "The lazy must be culled." I checked the bag, thinking maybe it was a Halloween promotion or something, but it was just a normal bag of cough drops. Besides, I bought this bag months ago. Probably just a printing mistake.

Tonight I continued the comics where I left off, getting through issue 30. They're more violent than I remember. Like for example, the scene in issue 25 when Agent Shadow kills Doctor Snakeheart. I could have sworn the actual death happened off-panel, but now there was a graphic depiction of Shadow decapitating Snakeheart with a katana.

The dialogue is harsher, too. I'm sure there wasn't this much cursing and blood before. I would have remembered that. But these aren't reprints, they're literally the same comics I read as a kid.

Wednesday, October 26 7:38 AM

I woke up in the middle of the night and noticed the closet light was on. The door was closed, but I could see the light along the bottom of the door. I thought it was a little odd because I never turn that light on. Actually, I wasn't sure if that closet even had a light. Maybe I brushed against the switch at some point. But I was still half-asleep, so I wasn't going to trust my memory. I briefly considered getting up and turning it off, but I was comfy and didn't want to wake myself all the way up. So I waste a little electricity, I'm not going to lose sleep over it, ha ha. I thought I heard the rat skitter in the walls one more time, just before I fell asleep.

This morning, as I was getting dressed, I remembered the light. Huh. No light switch I can see. I opened the closet door and looked around. Nope, there are definitely no lights in that closet. I'd be more worried, but I know I was pretty tired last night. I probably dreamed the whole thing.

Thursday, October 27 6:42 AM

I woke up in the middle of the night again. Once again, I saw a line of light glowing along the bottom of the closet door. This time I had to get to the bottom of it. I got out of bed and walked over to the door. As I reached for the door, I noticed the light became broken. At first I nearly jumped, thinking something was moving in there. Then I realized I was the one blocking the light. That's right, the light wasn't coming from underneath the door after all, it was just a beam of light landing at that particular spot, creating the illusion that it was coming from beneath the door.

I looked around for the source of the light, and found it right off. There's a guest room across the hall from my bedroom. The blinds in that room's window don't go quite all the way down to the sill, so there's a short horizontal gap where you can see outside. There's a particularly bright streetlamp outside that window - I swear it must be nuclear powered. Its light makes an almost laser-like horizontal beam that cuts across the hall, through both open doors, and ends up along the bottom of the bedroom closet. Crazy.

I don't like closing my bedroom door at night; it makes me feel too confined. But I stepped into the hallway and closed the door to the guest room. This broke the optical illusion, and I went back to bed.

I heard the rat again. I'll probably have to break down and buy some some poison. I'm just not sure where to put it where the rat can get to it.

Thursday, October 27 9:07 PM

I had to repeat myself a lot at work today, and I had

trouble understanding my coworkers as well. I don't know why. I don't think I was mumbling, and nobody here has any odd accents. At lunch I stopped at the nearby deli. The guy at the counter said something unintelligible that I assumed was "How are you today?"

I answered, "Not bad, and yourself?" He gave me a puzzled look and I realized he'd actually asked me for my order. Embarrassed, I told him I'd have the chicken salad.

"A chicken xalak?" he asked, raising an eyebrow. "What's a chicken xalak?" I repeated my order, slower, and he made my sandwich. As he wrapped it up, he said, "Punish them."

"What?"

"Here it comes," he said, sounding a little annoyed. I paid for my sandwich and left.

Friday, October 28 6:03 AM

Last night I had an unusual dream. It was, well, erotic. I haven't had THAT kind of dream since I was fifteen, but this one was intense. I was in the army barracks, talking to Agent Shadow from the Warzone comics. Dreams are weird - sometimes he looked animated, sometimes looked like a flesh-and-blood human. I've never seen a live-action Agent Shadow (was he even in the movies?) so my brain substituted a young Gary Sinise.

He was shirtless, but still wearing a hat. I felt the urge to apologize for staring, but he leaned over and kissed me. He opened my shirt and planted little kisses on my chest, gradually working his way down. Then he unzipped my pants and started pleasuring me. Within a couple of minutes I was spent. Then he raised his head and looked intently into my eyes.

He smiled, way too widely. His mouth opened to an unnatural degree, and then other mouths started opening on his neck. His chin enlarged, growing forward like a horse's snout. He closed his eyes, and his eyelids sealed shut, skin growing over until there was no sign that he'd ever had eyes. More mouths kept opening on the sides of his jaw, as his entire head grew and darkened. The mouths gibbered nonsensical words, sometimes chanting strange phrases in multiple languages. One mouth said, "Bring them to Xalak." I counted seventeen mouths by the time I jolted awake.

It was dark, but not as dark as it should have been. The closet light was on again. But... that didn't make sense. I'd closed the spare room's door before going to bed. There was nowhere that light could have come from. I heard that sound again, like a rat in the walls, but this time it seemed to be coming from the direction of the closet.

I shivered and pulled my blanket tighter around me. I was thirsty. My boxers were a sticky mess. I had to pee. But there was no way I was getting out of that bed. I held my eyes closed tight, trying to ignore the noise. I don't know how long I stayed like that, but I must have fallen asleep at some point because I had more dreams. I can't remember anything specific, just dark shapes.

Friday, October 28 8:52 PM

Work was nuts. I don't mean it was busy, I mean it was nuts. I had more and more trouble understanding people. They just weren't speaking English. I wrote an entire document, but when I reread it, it was just gibberish.

On the drive home, I saw strange things out of the corners of my eyes. I saw a troll running down the street, but when I turned to look at it, it was just a jogger. In the rearview mirror, it looked like a troll again. I thought I saw something in the back seat, but there was nothing there.

I stopped at a drive-thru window, but we barely understood each other. I said "No onions" and she replied "No survivors?" Onions doesn't even sound like survivors.

Saturday, October 29 1:29 AM

I can't sleep. I keep hearing the rats. I knocked holes in the wall, looking for them. Now I feel like they're watching at me through the holes.

I read a few more comics. Something is definitely different. Some of the characters have red eyes. Did someone deface my comics? Did I do that as a kid? The further I get into the series, the more the characters seem to look straight at the reader, as if breaking the fourth wall. I feel like they're staring at me, just like the rats.

Saturday, October 29 5:47 AM

When I tried to sleep again, the closet light had returned. I turned on the lamp, and the light went away. I looked out the bedroom door, confirming the spare room was closed. There was no light coming in from across the hall. I went back to bed, closed my eyes, and pulled the covers over my head. It took me an hour to fall asleep. I swear I could hear breathing.

Doctor Snakeheart visited me in my dream. This one wasn't a sex dream, though. We just sat and talked. He was super excited about a new torture device he'd constructed. Though the way he described it, it sounded too deadly for there to be much torture involved. Really, it sounded more like a human-sized meat grinder. They never would have gotten away with showing this machine in the comics.

We talked some more, but I can't remember much else. During the dream I understood him perfectly, but in trying to remember it the dialog sounds like he was talking through a trombone, like a cartoon schoolteacher. The last thing I remember is him telling me, "You must collect them… collect them for Xalak."

That makes sense. I'm experiencing a clarity now I've never had before. I'm no longer afraid. I know what I need to do.

Saturday, October 29 2:31 PM

Work work work. Trick-or-Treaters should be here tomorrow. I may not even sleep tonight, there's too much to do.

Sunday, October 30 5:22 AM

So, the route no longer just goes out the back door. Now there are two routes. Good children - the ones who love Halloween and wear cool costumes - get to go out the back door. Teenagers who don't wear costumes, using nasty pillowcases for candy, they get the new route. It leads from the front door, through my living room, down to my basement. There is no route back out. I've set up a special surprise down there.

A very special surprise. Doctor Snakeheart would be proud.

Traveler

Trex woke up in a strange bed. But then, when did they not? What even was "strange," when every day was so vastly different?

But this particular bed challenged that theory. The sheets and pillowcases were black and deep red. The headboard was black wood, carved with depictions of human skulls. The rest of the room was decorated in a similar style, with furniture that could have come right out of a vampire movie.

Was this entire world like this? Or had they just woken up in the house of a serial killer? And how had the previous Trex come to fall asleep here? Hoping for answers, Trex looked around the room. There was a piece of paper on the nightstand, with some writing on it.

Trex held up the paper, but couldn't read the words. This body was farsighted. They held the paper at arm's length, then noticed a pair of glasses on the nightstand. They put them on, and the words became clear.

Dear Trex,

Hope you're not too freaked out. This was a strange day. Apparently this kid's into goth shit. Don't worry, the rest of the world's not like this. After school, take a walk around town. It's nice. But be back for dinner; the mother is a great cook. This Trex seems pretty well taken care of, so you won't have to get a day job or anything. Try not to piss off their stepfather, and you'll be fine.

Love, Trex

It wasn't the worst world they'd been to, not by far. Just last week they'd woken up in a bed of snow, chilled to the bone. And yesterday they'd had to deal with all those mosquitos. They felt sorry for the Trex who took over that body today, they were going to spend the entire day scratching bug bites.

Trex got up, found some clothes on the floor, and put them on. The bedroom had its own bathroom, and when they were done in there, they took a long look in the mirror. It was the third day in a row they'd been female. This one was of Asian descent, late teens. Short black hair, pierced eyebrows. A tattoo of a skull on the left cheek.

Not bad, Trex thought. In the past three years, they'd been in every body imaginable. They didn't really have a lot of preferences. Gender meant nothing to them anymore, and race was just pigment. But this Trex looked like a badass, and it would be fun walking around in their skin for the day.

"Trex, breakfast!" they heard from downstairs. Trex took one last look in the mirror to make sure they were dressed appropriately, then walked out the door.

It had been three years since that field trip to the Large Hadron Collider, and the freak lightning storm that had apparently occurred in all universes simultaneously. Now, somehow, every Trex in every universe was connected. Every morning, new body. Never the same one twice. They had to figure out where the previous Trex had left off, and try not to let their friends and family know anything was different.

That last one wasn't universal – no aspect of this

arrangement was. Sometimes the parents and friends knew their Trex had been going through something. More than once Trex had woken up in a mental institution. Other times they were in a hostile family environment, with parents that accused them of faking it for attention. But a lot of the Trex's had somehow managed to go the three years – that's over one thousand different minds – without their family or friends knowing there was a problem.

Well, that wasn't entirely true. Of course people had noticed their erratic behavior. They'd lost friends and jobs, and nobody thought they were "normal," whatever that meant. But Trex was still amazed at how many of their counterparts still lived a relatively conventional life. A thousand transfers and no one had blown their cover?

But the reason why was obvious. While the different versions of Trex had their own personalities, they all had a shared self-interest. As long as each Trex tried to keep life as normal as possible for the next Trex, then together they all benefited as a whole. Not all of them were on the same page there, though. Trex had woken up in plenty of bodies that were suffering the effects of the previous night's debauchery. Trex really wished they could ask their other selves just what they were thinking. But their only means of communication was to leave notes for the following Trex. There just wasn't any way to contact the previous Trex.

Hopefully, somehow, they would all end up in their original bodies someday. Trex had a theory about that. When the universe ran out of different versions of Trex, and each Trex wound up in their original body, maybe, just maybe, the cycle would end. The idea being that the reason they switched every night was because the universe was still trying to fix the original mistake. Each time a Trex wound up in the right body, it would lock in place and be taken out of rotation.

Okay, maybe it wasn't a theory so much as wishful thinking.

How many transfers would it take? Trex had thoughts on

that as well. If there were an infinite number of universes, then things looked pretty grim. But even if there were, only some of them had Large Hadron Supercolliders, and only a subset of those had someone named Trex visit the Supercollider on that fateful day approximately three years earlier.

The answer was still incalculable without more data. Obviously it was more than a thousand. But how much more? That was the question.

The previous Trex had been right about their mother. Breakfast was delicious. The only thing that marred the experience was this Trex's stepfather, who kept looking at them in ways that seemed inappropriate. He wasn't even being subtle about it, and Trex was amazed that their mother hadn't noticed.

Or perhaps she had, but she'd had the objections beaten out of her. The way she served her husband breakfast, it seemed like she was walking on eggshells, afraid that if it wasn't perfect, there would be consequences. But he seemed too busy concentrating on Trex to even notice what he was eating.

After breakfast, Trex asked their mom if there was anything she needed, and was told, "No, sweetie, enjoy your day at school."

Trex found their bookbag packed up and ready to go, and they resolved to do the same thing later that evening so the next day's Trex wouldn't have to go looking for their books. There was even a helpful sheet of paper in the bag, which told Trex which rooms to go to for which class periods. It even had a map to the school. It was only a couple of blocks away, and the walk took about ten minutes.

First period was math, and there was a test. Trex was lucky, in their original world they were in college on a science scholarship, so high school algebra was a breeze for them. They wondered how many of their counterparts had felt totally out of their element when waking up with Trex's original life, which they thought of as "Trex Prime." What was going on with Trex Prime right now? They'd probably dropped out of college. If high school students had been taking their classes, Prime had probably been booted out of school by now. They'd have to do a lot of damage control if – when – everyone got back where they should be.

The next two classes were easy as well. Then came lunch, which was more challenging. There were no empty tables, so Trex had to sit next to someone. Picking the wrong person could have had serious repercussions for this Trex's social life. They spotted an empty seat next to a girl that looked to be about this Trex's age, and sat down. The girl glanced at Trex, rolled her eyes, then went back to talking to her friends.

Good enough, Trex thought, and ate their lunch. No one spoke to them while they ate, but being invisible was one of the better outcomes right now. Trex looked around the room to see if maybe someone else was beckoning to them to join them, but no one even looked in Trex's direction. Actually, that wasn't true. There was a boy, probably seventeen or eighteen. He had a pierced eyebrow and green hair. He kept glancing at Trex, then looking away.

When Trex was done eating, they got up to use the restroom. They almost went into the boys room – it was hard to keep track sometimes – but then turned toward the girls. Before they could go in, however, they felt a hand on their shoulder. It was the green-haired boy.

"Trex," he said. "Look, I have something to say. Um… okay?"

Trex said nothing and just nodded for him to continue.

"Look," he said again. "I know it's been a few years since we broke up, but I still care about you. You know?"

"Thank you," Trex said. They looked him up and down for red flags, maybe signs they'd been in an abusive relationship. But other than his punk aesthetic, he seemed harmless so far.

"I know something's up with you," he said. "You don't have friends anymore. From what I hear, your grades are all over the place. Ace one test, flunk the next one. You used to be an honor student."

"I've been... going through some things," Trex said.

"You remember my sister, right?" the boy said.

Trex nodded again, hoping there were no follow-up questions.

"She acted just like you, right before she, you know," he said. "I know the signs. Please, if you have anything you want to talk about, just tell me."

Trex smiled, then kissed him on the cheek. "Thank you, I'll keep that in mind," they said. Then they turned and headed into the restroom. They weren't sure if the kiss had been appropriate, but this Trex might need more people like that boy in their life.

After school, Trex decided to follow the previous Trex's advice and take a walk around town. It was an idyllic little neighborhood, where everything was within walking distance. There was a shopping center right across the street from the school, with a soda shop that looked right out of the 1950s. Now that they thought about it, a lot of the fashions they'd seen in school had also seemed a bit retro. Even the cars driving by had a classic vibe to their designs.

But the technology was modern. As Trex took a seat in the soda shop, their smartphone buzzed. They'd received a text from their stepfather. Trex unlocked their phone. It was odd, but every Trex used the same PIN. Some things just seemed universal across all the different worlds.

The text read, "Be home by 7. Your mother has a nice dinner planned."

Trex replied, "Looking forward to it." It was currently just a little after three, so they'd have plenty of time to look around town.

As long as the phone was unlocked, Trex started going through the photos, hoping to glean any context they could to get through the day. They saw a few pictures of this Trex with their friends. Trex had seen some of those girls in school earlier, but they hadn't given Trex the time of day. The girls in the photos looked a bit younger, so Trex checked the dates. The photos were dated three years earlier, from before the accident.

A server in a poodle dress showed up and took Trex's order. They ordered a strawberry milkshake, hoping they'd like it. That was another problem with switching bodies all the time. Some foods just tasted different to other Trex's taste buds. Or maybe food actually tasted different on other worlds. Who's to say every universe uses the same recipe for strawberry milkshakes? For that matter, strawberries in this world might have evolved to taste like onions.

Trex winced at the thought of an onion milkshake and continued to flip through the photos. They were sorted by oldest first, so they scrolled to the bottom to look at some more recent shots. Sometimes their counterparts took helpful pics and added captions so that their future selves wouldn't have to guess so much. Some even made use of their phone's notepad software. But most Trex's just tried to get through their day.

They found a few helpful pictures of classmates, with captions. The green-haired boy's name was "Billy," though he had black hair in the photo. There was a blonde girl named "Cassie," and a dark-haired girl named "Vespa," both of whom Trex had seen in class. Maybe they should have tried to sit with them during lunch, but who knew if they were still on speaking terms?

The server returned with the milkshake, and Trex took a long sip. It was wonderful. They continued to flip through the photos until they found one that made them choke on their milkshake. They quickly hid the phone in their lap to hide the disgusting image from anyone who might be looking in their direction. When they were done coughing, they looked around to make sure no one was watching, and looked at the photo again.

The picture showed Trex's current self. They were nude, and the picture showed them from the navel up, from a low angle. Someone was standing behind them. It looked like a man, but only their arms were visible in the photo. The arms groped Trex from behind. It looked like a selfie, but Trex had been holding the camera low, perhaps to keep the person behind them from seeing they were taking the pic. It was hard to read Trex's expression from this angle, but they didn't look happy.

"What'cha looking at?"

The voice startled Trex so much they dropped the phone, then dove for it before anyone could see the picture. Then they banged their head on the table trying to stand up.

"Sorry I scared you, you okay?"

Trex sat back in their seat. Billy sat across the table from them, a concerned look on his face.

"Hey, Billy," Trex said.

"You never called me that before," he said.

Trex had to stop themself from asking what they usually called him. "So, what brings you here?" they asked.

"I always stop here after school," Billy said. "My dad owns the place, you know that."

"Right, I forgot," Trex replied.

"I'm lying," Billy said. "I saw you through the window. And you know I've never met my dad. Seriously, what's going on with you?"

"I couldn't even begin to explain it," Trex said.

"Whatever it is, I want to help you," Billy said.

Trex stared at him. "You just want to get back together."

"If it's in the cards, sure," Billy said. "I won't lie about that. But even if we don't, I want to be there for you. I don't want you to end up like my sister. She... she thought she was alone in the world. I never want you to feel that way."

Trex put their hand on Billy's and smiled. This was a bad idea. Trex resolved early on not to mess with anyone's relationships, lest they find themselves in tricky situations whenever things went back to normal. But perhaps if this Trex had someone to confide in, it would make it easier for future inhabitants of this body to get through their day.

They wouldn't tell Billy the real truth, that was right out. But some believable lie, something that would explain the daily personality changes and forgetfulness. The question boiled down to, should they trust this person?

"All right," Trex said. "Come to my house around nine, and I'll tell you everything." That would give them time to come up with a believable story, and they could leave the details in their phone for the next Trex.

"I'll be there," Billy said. Then he kissed Trex on the hand, stood up, and left.

While Trex finished off their milkshake, they resumed looking through the phone. There weren't any other incriminating photos, so they switched to the phone's notepad program. It was chock full of useful notes that Trex probably should have looked through as soon as they'd gotten up in the morning. Some of it was redundant with the gallery and the paper notes. Directions to the school, the room numbers for their classes, some notes about some of their friends.

But one note really stood out. Short and sweet, in nice, big letters it read: DON'T TRUST WILLIAM

Trex no longer felt like exploring the town. They'd probably regret missing the opportunity later, but they decided to head home. As soon as they walked in the door, they went upstairs and breezed through their homework, thinking about Billy the entire time. They set up their schoolbag so the next day's Trex wouldn't have to worry about it. Then it was time for dinner, which was even tastier than breakfast had been.

After dinner, Trex went up to their room. A million thoughts swirled through their mind. Billy. William. Was he the one from the lewd photo? If Trex confided in him, would he keep the secret? What should they even tell him?

There was a knock at the door. Trex's stepfather came in. Trex was confused when they saw him lock the door behind himself.

"What's up?" Trex asked.

His eyes were all over them, and never in Trex's lives had someone's intentions been so obvious. He smiled, a smile that sent shivers up Trex's spine.

"W-Where's mom?" Trex asked.

"Bingo night," their stepfather said. "She'll be gone for hours." He put his hand on Trex's shoulder.

"What are you..." Trex started to say, but the question became meaningless as he slipped his other hand around Trex's waist.

"I'll tell everyone," Trex said.

"I don't think you will," their stepfather said. "See, I'm onto you. You can't keep memories from one day to the next. You're like that girl in that Adam Sadler movie."

Sandler, Trex thought. Though it was perfectly possible the actor's name was Sadler in this universe.

"I figured it out a couple of years ago," he continued. "You try to cover it up, but I can tell you're faking. I've even helped you a few times. Kept you from seeing a shrink. The bottom line is, I can do anything I want, as long as I drug you to sleep afterward."

"You won't get away with this," Trex said. They tried to pull out of the man's grip, but he was too strong.

"You have no idea how many times I've already gotten away with it. There's a reason I look forward to your mother's bingo night."

The thought made Trex sick to their stomach. How many of Trex's counterparts had this man raped while in this body? There were probably dozens of them living with that horrible memory, now worlds away where they were too busy facing new challenges to find closure. At least the Trex who came from this world wouldn't have to live with that knowledge, but that didn't make it any better.

There was a knock at the window, and Billy's face appeared in the glass. Trex's stepfather tossed them aside and ran to the window. Then he opened the window and immediately put his hands around Billy's neck.

Trex looked around for a weapon and found a replica katana on the wall. The sword wasn't sharp, but Trex's stepfather still screamed when it came down on top of his head. He released Billy and turned back to Trex, his face full of fury. A bit of blood dribbled down his forehead. "I'll kill you," he said.

Trex took another swing, but their stepfather caught the blade in his hand. If it hurt, he didn't seem to notice. He yanked the sword from Trex's hand, then tossed it aside. He reached for Trex with both hands.

Then suddenly he was gone, yanked backward out the window. Trex ran to the window and looked down. Billy hung from the trellis with one hand, and Trex's stepfather lay on the ground down below. He wasn't moving.

They waited until Trex's mom came home to call the police. Trex and Billy explained the situation to her – minus the sci-fi elements – and she had no trouble believing them. "It's all my fault," Trex's mother said. "William's been abusing me for years. I should have known he'd go after you. I never should have left you two alone in the house together."

"It's not your fault, mom," Trex said. "But there's another problem. I've... been having memory problems lately."

"I know," their mother said. "You've told me before. One time you even tried to convince me you were from another dimension. I wanted to send you to a psychiatrist, but William wouldn't let me. So I've been doing my best to keep your life as stable as possible. Obviously I wasn't doing enough."

"The point is," Trex continued, "I might not remember any of this happened tomorrow. Whatever you tell the police, I won't be able to corroborate it."

"I can," Billy said. "I saw him attack you through the window."

"Neither of you need to worry," Trex's mother said. "I've been saving up evidence for years. And if they don't believe me, we'll cross that bridge when we come to it. I'm just glad he'll never hurt anyone else."

Trex and their mother hugged, then called the police.

That night, Trex updated the notes in their phone, then put it in the charger. Then they crumpled up the previous Trex's note and threw it in the trash, and wrote out their own.

Trex–

This is a nice town, explore it if you get a chance. Billy is good company. He and your mother both think you have memory issues, so just go with it. Your stepfather recently died. Don't feel bad, he was not a nice person. Enjoy your mother's cooking.

-Trex

They placed the note on the nightstand, turned off the lights, and went to sleep. They didn't know what tomorrow would bring, but after today, they were ready for anything.

Justice

"One more for the road, good lady." The customer placed another ten dollar bill on the counter. He gave the bartender a smarmy grin, his blue eyes looking her up and down like he was appraising a piece of jewelry.

Shiela gave him her biggest, fakest smile, then turned to make the drink. It had been an uncomfortable couple of hours, and she would be glad to see this customer leave. She couldn't even put her finger on why. The man was charming enough, and a big tipper. But he also gave off a vibe – nothing distinct, nothing obvious – but Sheila was glad he wasn't the only customer in the bar. She wouldn't want to be alone with this guy.

Still, she had her part to play. "Here you go, sugar," she said, setting down the fresh drink and picking up the money. "Any change back?"

"It's all yours," the man said, taking a sip of his fourth screwdriver. "I've got lots to celebrate tonight."

"That right?" Sheila asked, though the last thing she wanted was to hear this story. Guys like him were so predictable. He'd tell her some made-up tale about how he'd just won the lottery, or got a promotion, or that his wealthy uncle had left him a large sum of money. If Sheila sounded even a little bit impressed, the guy would ask her what time she got off work. Then she'd have to mention her boyfriend –

118

not that she had one – and hopefully the customer would back off.

Unfortunately, the boyfriend trick didn't always work. More than once she'd been locking up and spotted someone waiting for her in the parking lot. She was lucky, though. She had a trick most women didn't have, and it had saved her several times.

The customer was talking, but Sheila only half-listened, nodding her head occasionally. She didn't want to appear too interested. He was saying something about getting falsely accused, going to court, and finally winning the case. It was only when he mentioned a specific name that Sheila snapped to attention.

"Did you say Goldstein?" Sheila asked, and the man nodded. She looked around behind the bar, finally coming up with a newspaper. "This is you?" she asked, pointing to an article. The headline read:

PARADISE ACQUITTED DUE TO LACK OF EVIDENCE

"Oh, look, I'm famous," the man said with a half-smile.

"You're Jason Paradise," Sheila said, glowering. "The rapist."

"Not according to the courts," he said.

"Three different women claim you coerced them into sex with you," Sheila said.

"Liars, all of them," Jason said. His expression darkened. "*They* seduced *me*. They got what they wanted, then they teamed up and had me arrested. They figured they could get a few bucks out of me."

"They said you have superpowers," Sheila said. "Hypnotic eyes that prevented them from saying no." Six years earlier, a radioactive meteor hit Cleveland. Roughly a third of the Earth's population had since developed superpowers, though most of these powers were useless. For every person who gained the power of flight or invulnerability, a thousand people were stuck with little tricks, like the ability to change the color of their fingernails or a knack for predicting when a gallon of milk would go bad.

"Like I said, liars," Jason said. "They were jealous of each other, and tried to take it out on me."

Sheila made a point of looking at the bar instead of his face. "I think you should leave," she said.

"Look me in the eyes and say that," Jason said.

"Leave or I'll call the cops," Sheila said.

"Go ahead, they'll be on my side," he said, his voice slurring a little.

Out of the corner of her eye, Sheila could see him leaning closer, trying to move into her field of vision. She turned farther away.

"Oops," Jason said, and there was a crash of glass breaking. Sheila involuntarily looked up, briefly catching his gaze. His eyes had a shimmering quality to them. The blue of his irises seemed to undulate like waves on the ocean. Sheila couldn't look away. "I seem to have dropped my glass," Jason said.

"That's okay," Sheila heard herself say. She couldn't get over how beautiful this man was. How had she not seen it before? His sandy-blond mullet was perfectly combed, and it really complemented his five o'clock shadow. Sheila wasn't into men, but there was something about this guy that made her want to lock up early and see what was under that cheap suit.

You're smarter than this, she thought. *He's using his power on you.* But that part of her brain wasn't currently in charge of her body. She found herself leaning in closer, as if she might kiss him right then and there.

He put his hand on her arm, and for a split second, that broke the spell. Thinking fast, Sheila used her own power. Shockwaves of electricity coursed over her body, and Jason was thrown backward onto the floor. Covering her eyes with her hand, Sheila shouted, "Get out of my bar or I'll call the cops!" A couple of the other patrons stood up from their seats and started to walk over.

"I'll sue you for this," Jason said, clumsily getting to his feet.

"Is he bothering you?" another customer asked. It was Carter, one of her regulars. He was a burly truck driver who liked telling bad jokes. But right now he was dead serious.

"Just get him out of here," Sheila said, still not looking in Jason's direction.

"I'll go, I'll go," Jason said, backing away from the other customers. "I know when I'm not wanted." He turned and walked out the door.

Sheila had to sit down for a minute. Carter helped her over to a table, where she sat with her head in her hands. "Why are people like this?" she asked aloud. There had to be a ton of altruistic and profitable uses for Jason's powers. He could have been a motivational speaker, a hostage negotiator, or maybe even a therapist. But he'd chosen to use his power for self-gratification, not caring who he hurt.

That was the problem with society. The overlap between "people who want to fix the world" and "people who have the power to change the world" was virtually nil. The majority of the population was at the mercy of a few, and those few rarely acted beyond their own self-interests. Even the truly selfless superheroes, like Justice Lass and Captain Virtue, only fought to protect the status quo.

Would anyone ever come along with both the will and the power to enact true change?

Jason stumbled through the dark alley beside the bar. He'd had more to drink than he'd thought. Fuzzy images swirled through his mind, mostly revenge scenarios involving that prudish bartender and her other customers. He stopped and leaned against the wall, trying to remember where he'd parked the car. He knew he should call a cab, but he didn't want to have to come back for his car later. Besides, this wouldn't be the drunkest he'd ever driven.

He vaguely remembered parking it on the street, half a block down. He was about to start walking again, but first he needed to take a piss. He lurched forward until he found a spot beside a trash bin, where he was mostly obscured by shadow. He put one hand against the wall and unzipped his pants with the other. He felt immediate relief as he loosed his bladder on the concrete.

Something brushed against his leg, making him jump. It was just a cat, with orange-striped fur. "Lousy stray," he mumbled, nudging it away with his leg. He'd always been more of a dog person.

When he was done peeing, he zipped up his pants, tried to remember which way he'd been walking, and ambled in that direction. Another cat, this one black and white, approached him and meowed. Jason tried to kick it, but missed by a mile, and nearly lost his balance.

Neither of the cats fled, and they were joined by five more. "Whaddya want?" Jason said, trying to focus his eyes. "I don't have any food." With his double vision there were at least fourteen cats. And soon there were. More cats poured into the alley, coming in from both ends, some climbing down from the bar's roof.

Jason kept walking forward, but soon he was pushing through a sea of cats, and the end of the alley just kept getting further away. At first the strays seemed friendly, but suddenly, all at once, they started hissing at him. "What is this?" Jason said in exasperation.

As if in response, the cats swarmed over him, climbing up his body, dragging him to the ground. They scratched him over and over, and all Jason could do was cover his eyes with his hands. *Can I really die this way?* he wondered. *Death by a thousand cuts?* The cats couldn't scratch him very deep, but some of the cuts were large enough to cause concern. One good swipe across his throat and he'd be done for.

No! he thought. *I won't go out like this.* He defiantly rose to his feet, kicking and throwing cats left and right. He stumbled again, and nearly went back down, but he stood his ground. As if he was crossing a raging river, he took slow steps forward, stomping his way through the frenzied swarm. He was less than fifteen feet from the street when he heard a low growl from somewhere behind him. He turned for a look, then froze in place.

Standing at the far end of the alley, another cat-shaped silhouette stared at him. Only this one was larger, much larger. As it came more into focus, he recognized the brown-and-white markings of a cougar. Jason stepped back, tripping over several cats and landing on his back. He tried to sit up, but cats were already swarming over his chest. He managed to look up just in time to see the cougar pounce.

The Museum of Cultural Acquisitions wasn't exactly a fortress, but it still had decent security. Instead of night watchmen, it had a huge number of video cameras, laser alarm systems, and electronic locks. And all of it could be controlled by a single computer in the manager's office.

Another thing it had? A garbage chute. The museum's cafeteria on the second floor produced a lot of waste, and the kitchen featured a chute that led directly into the trash bin behind the building. The chute wasn't quite wide enough for a human, or it might have been locked.

No one was around to see the chute open by itself. No one saw the small gray tabby climb out and hop to the floor, right before making a beeline to the office. If anyone had been around to witness the intrusion, they would have been impressed by the cat's ability to avoid security cameras and lasers. They'd have been more impressed to see the cat leap up and twist the doorknob between its paws, allowing it to enter the manager's office. But most of all, they would have been astounded when the cat jumped up onto the manager's desk, switched on the computer, and tapped out the password with its paws.

All around the museum, cameras and lasers turned off.

Doors unlocked all over the building, and automatic doors slid open. A woman entered the museum from the backdoor, followed by a few hundred cats. The woman had long black hair and wore a black leather outfit that wouldn't have looked out of place at a bondage club.

As she walked through the museum's various wings, the swarm of cats gradually diminished as smaller groups split off. Many retrieved small relics and rushed them outside, depositing them in the woman's van. Some cats worked together to carry larger objects. None of them had to be given any orders, as they seemed to have their missions memorized.

As for the woman herself, she had a specific target in mind, something that couldn't be carried by house cats. The cougar walked beside her as she approached an ancient stone tablet. She reached out for the artifact, then froze when another woman's voice spoke behind her. "You know, they sell replicas in the museum gift shop."

Mistress Clowder turned around and recognized her adversary right away. Justice Lass floated a few feet above the floor in her iconic red, white, and blue cheerleader costume. Her blonde hair and miniskirt ruffled in the breeze, even though the air was still. "Are you actually using your powers to move your hair?" Clowder asked.

"It's a side effect of my flight," Justice Lass answered. "It creates a field of static electricity. You should see how much I spend on dryer sheets. Do you want to banter some more, or get straight to the fight?"

"Oh, I'll take the banter any day," Clowder purred. "It's half the fun. Once we start fighting, it's just Pow! Bam! Crunch! ...and then I'm off to prison again. But something tells me you're not here to protect a few dusty artifacts. Don't you usually concentrate on more dangerous villains?" Cats continued to pass them in both directions, some dragging priceless antiquities with their mouths.

Justice Lass nodded. "Have you heard of a man named

Jason Paradise?"

"The rapist?" Clowder spat. "Last I heard, his case was dismissed."

"He was found dead in an alley last night," Justice Lass said. "Covered in claw marks."

"And what does that have to do with me?" Clowder asked, looking at her fingernails.

"Seriously?" Justice Lass asked. When Mistress Clowder didn't say anything, she continued. "You're the only one in the city who can control large numbers of cats. The victim's wounds—"

"The victim?" Clowder asked, suddenly furious. "Did you dare call that man a victim? That man ruined lives. What happened to him was karma, pure and simple." Then she calmed down. "Besides, I can account for my whereabouts last night. I have witnesses and everything."

"Which proves nothing," Justice Lass said. "Everyone knows you can control cats at long distances."

"That still isn't evidence," Clowder said. "You can punch through brick walls. Does that make you the first suspect every time someone is found bashed to death? Maybe someone in town has powers like mine, and they just haven't gone public yet. Or maybe—"

"That's enough," Justice Lass interrupted. "I'm taking you to the police. If you're innocent, you can officially prove it to them."

"Fine, fine," Clowder said. "But before you do, let me ask you a question. There's probably a natural disaster going on somewhere right now. Why do you think it's worth your time to defend a man whose death made the world a safer place?"

"Because I believe in justice," the hero answered.

"Do you though?" Clowder asked. "Was it really 'justice' what happened in that trial yesterday? Surely you don't believe that our so-called legal system is the end-all-be-all of justice." Seven cats worked together to drag an entire mummy down the hall, but the two women only stared at each other.

Justice Lass paused. "It has its flaws," she finally admitted. "But our laws keep society functioning. And where do you get off lecturing me about laws while you're actively robbing a museum?"

"I'm not robbing anything," Mistress Clowder said. "I'm returning previously-stolen artifacts to their countries of origin."

"For a fee," Justice Lass said.

"My time is valuable," Mistress Clowder replied. "And there is some personal risk involved. But I assure you, I took this job for altruistic reasons."

Justice Lass opened her mouth to respond, but paused. A look of doubt crossed her face. After a few more seconds of thought, she said, "Says the woman in BDSM gear."

"Personal attacks don't help your argument," Clowder replied. "In fact, they just prove you don't have anything substantial to say. Besides, I won't take fashion advice from someone who flies around in a miniskirt. Tell me, do you get a perverse thrill from flaunting your undies to the world?"

"Okay, that's a common misconception," Justice Lass said. "First off, this is a leotard. I'm wearing more underwear underneath it. The outfit would look perfectly decent without the skirt at all, but I like the skirt because of the way it flows in the wind. Besides, the skirt actually gives me an extra layer of modesty, and keeps people from staring at my butt all the time."

"Wow, I think I struck a nerve," Clowder said. "But my position still stands. It isn't justice when rapists and murderers walk free. It isn't justice when people steal historical artifacts from other countries. It isn't justice when billionaires hoard more wealth than they could possibly spend in a hundred lifetimes, while most people can't make their rent. You tell yourself you stand for justice, but you're really just an enabler for a corrupt government that grants more rights to those who can pay for them."

"That's not fair," Justice Lass said. "We have free elections. If you don't like the system the way it is, vote until it's better."

"That's a joke," Clowder said. "Every election cycle it's the same thing. The guy who's pure evil versus the guy who won't be able to get anything done. Meanwhile, misinformation spreads so fast, most voters don't realize they're voting against their own best interests."

"I know the system's not perfect, but—"

"Not perfect?" Clowder shouted. "It's not even adequate. Not by a long shot. And you go flying around with your hands on your hips, convinced that you're the embodiment of justice, when all you really do is protect the barriers between the poor and the rich."

"Now hold on—" Justice Lass said.

"No," Clowder said. "You had your chance to help people, but you became a propaganda machine instead. A symbol without a soul. Sure, you've saved a few lives, but by your inaction, you've condemned thousands more to homelessness and starvation."

Justice Lass looked confused. She wanted to counter all of Clowder's arguments, but every retort she considered sounded hollow.

Finally Mistress Clowder broke the silence. "Are you going to arrest me or not?"

"I don't... know," Justice Lass said. "Tell me more about these artifacts."

"Let's sit down and talk," Mistress Clowder said, and led her to a bench.

One month later...

Braxton Blount was the eighth richest man on the planet. His ability to predict the stock market bordered on the supernatural, and many speculated it was the result of that power-granting meteor. He now owned one of the world's largest retail chains, as well as the factories that produced its wares. His net worth measured in the billions, and yet most of his employees struggled to afford groceries. Some people might have wondered how he slept at night. The answer? On a bed so soft, it was like sleeping on a cloud.

At least, that's where he'd fallen asleep. As he started to wake up, he realized that he wasn't in his bed. He wasn't in a bed at all, but in some sort of leather seat. He opened his eyes and saw a sky full of stars… and the Earth.

The last bit of sleep instantly faded as he tried to figure out where he was. He was belted into a pilot's chair, and there were blinking lights all around him. Straight ahead, the curved window revealed the infinite wonders of space. He tried to stand, straining against his harness. Then he unbuckled the restraints and leaned toward the glass.

"What is happening?" he shouted. He reached out and touched the glass canopy. From his new vantage point against the glass, he could see the surrounding landscape. Whatever sort of vehicle he was in, it was parked on the moon.

"Oh good, you're awake," a woman's voice said.

Braxton craned his neck, looking for the source. He was still incredibly disoriented. He felt like he'd been drugged at some point, because that heavy, medicinal feeling still hung around his head. Finally his eyes fell on the two women standing behind him. He recognized both right off. One was the Robin Hood-esque supervillain, Mistress Clowder, wearing her usual NSFW outfit. The other was the paragon of truth, Justice Lass. Except she was harder to recognize because instead of her usual patriotic getup, she now wore a black uniform. The two held hands in a way that seemed beyond mere friendship, in Braxton's estimation.

"Are we on the moon?" Braxton asked. In truth, it always had been a dream of his to visit the moon. With his fortune, he was one of the few people on Earth who could have made it happen. Other than actual astronauts, of course. But it had always seemed like a dangerous undertaking, and he enjoyed his life too much to risk losing it all.

"We are," Clowder replied.

"Why?" Braxton asked.

"Because we want to talk to you," Justice Lass said. "And we had to be sure we wouldn't be interrupted."

"And because we didn't want you to think about running off before we were done talking," Clowder added.

"And what makes you think I'm going to listen to a couple of kidnappers?" Braxton asked, his eyes narrowing.

"Because if we don't come to an equitable arrangement," Justice Lass said, "we might just go back home without you."

Blackmail, then, Braxton thought. "Fine," he said. "We'll talk. What's the subject?"

"Justice," Mistress Clowder said.

Sheila turned another chair upside-down and set it on the table. The last customer had left, the doors were locked, and she took her time cleaning up the place. The TV was still on, and Sheila watched the news as she put up the chairs and swept the floors.

The top story involved a billionaire named Braxton Blount. Apparently he'd had some sort of Scrooge-like epiphany and wanted to devote the remainder of his life to helping others. He'd decided to donate more than ninety percent of his wealth to programs that built tiny homes for the poor. Even his own sprawling mansion would soon be converted into an apartment complex for the homeless, while Braxton moved somewhere more sensible.

Good for him, Sheila thought. *Maybe this will become a trend. What a world this would be if the super-wealthy competed to see who could help the most people, instead of trying to outdo each other with their ostentatious possessions. Maybe the next billionaire will try to fix world hunger or make drugs available for those who can't afford them. Is that too much to ask?*

In the coming months, her musings would be answered in ways the world never dreamt possible.

Mutiny

"Come out with your hands up! We probably have you outnumbered!"

There was a pause, then a woman's voice called out from the dark corridor. "Did you say probably?"

Sergeant Stearnes cleared his throat before answering. "Honestly? I didn't see how many of you went in. With the lights out, and all that smoke, there could be three of you or thirty."

"Is this your first negotiation?" the ex-prisoner called from the darkness.

"...but I know this," the sergeant continued. "That corridor is a dead end. You're unarmed, and we have flamethrowers. If you come out now, we'll be happy to take you back to your cells. Otherwise we fill that corridor with flame. This little prison break of yours is over."

"I'm not, though," the woman called back.

The sergeant replayed the last couple of sentences in his mind. "You're not what?"

"Unarmed," the woman called back. "I took an jolt gun off one of the guards."

Stearnes rolled his eyes. "Whatever. You're still no a match for our firepower. Surrender now and—"

"I just wanted to let you know," the woman said. "Because I don't want you to shoot me for holding a weapon."

"Fine," the sergeant said. "Drop your weapon and come out with your hands above your head."

"But you don't know how many of us are in here," the woman said. "If I leave the weapon behind, you might think there's still an armed escapee here in the corridor. You might flame us just to be sure."

Is this woman thick or what? the sergeant wondered. "Very well," he said. "If it'll make you feel better, set the gun on the floor and slide it out to me. Then come out with your hands up."

"Okay, give me one moment," the woman said.

They heard a quiet clink in the corridor, then the pistol slid into view. Stearnes placed his foot on the gun as it came to a rest. "Good," he said. "Now, will you please just—"

"Whoops," the woman said. "Sorry, I accidentally activated the gun's self-destruct feature."

Stearnes lifted his foot. A little blue light blinked rapidly on the pistol. "Duck!" the sergeant ordered, and his soldiers jumped to the side. But they were too late. The weapon exploded, killing the sergeant and three of his guards.

The two remaining guards rushed to the corridor's entrance and fired blindly into the dark. After roughly ten seconds of continuous fire, they paused. Everything was quiet.

Then two bolts of energy flew out from the darkness, each unerringly finding its target. The guards went down instantly.

"Take their weapons," Zeta said, emerging from the corridor along with three men. "And follow me. We have an army to grow."

For the next half hour, Zeta and her companions released more prisoners from their cells. They fought off guards every step of the way, leaving none alive. "That's the last cell on this level," Deek said. He was a balding man in his fifties, with green eyes and weathered features.

Zeta surveyed her army. Fifty-six men stood in the corridor, and roughly a third of them were now armed. "Good," she said, brushing a lock of raven-black hair from her eyes. "Now for the hard part. A few of you are coming with me to the bridge. Most of you will go down to deck three and release the rest of the prisoners. Then we'll—"

Zeta's plans were interrupted by the ship's intercom. "Attention, prisoners! This is Captain Hartek. You will return to your cells or I will flood the prison levels with poisonous gas. You have sixty seconds."

"Bluffing," Zeta said.

"How do you know?" Deek asked.

"Because I used to work here," Zeta said.

"Not good enough," one of the prisoners said, raising his weapon on Zeta. Two of the other prisoners did the same. "I say we get back to our cells."

"Forty-four... forty-three... forty-two..." the captain's voice said.

"No," Zeta said. "This ship is taking us to Planet Bastille. We're going to be worked to death, if not executed outright. Do you think they're going to go easy on us all of a sudden because we went back to our cells? They're even madder at us now than they were before."

"Twenty-eight... twenty-seven... twenty-six..."

"Anything can happen between now and then," a prisoner said, holding his pistol higher.

"I know," Zeta said. "The gas is now, the execution is later. Of course you're more afraid of the immediate threat. But we're not going to have this opportunity again. If we give up now, we *will* die."

"Nine... eight... seven..."

The prisoner looked like he was about to pull the trigger, but then he lowered his weapon. "You better be right," he said.

"Two... one..."

Everyone held their breath.

The captain sounded annoyed when he spoke again. "Fine, you got me. We don't have any poison gas. But I absolutely will disable this ship's life support systems and evacuate my crew. This is your last chance. Surrender or perish."

Zeta smirked. "Stick with the plan," she said, and pointed at a small group of men. "You six, you're with me. The rest of you head down to the women's detention level."

"Get into your pod, that's an order!" Captain Hartek had to physically push his first officer through the escape hatch.

"I can't leave you alone—" Commander Greene replied, but the hatch slid shut behind him. Before he had a chance to turn around, he felt the pod vibrate as it was launched from the bridge.

"You too, Lamar," Hartek said, gesturing toward his security officer. "No arguments."

"Captain, it is my duty to protect you from—"

"That sounds like an argument," Hartek said. "You *will* get into that pod. That's an order."

Lamar stood firm. "I will not."

"Damn it," the captain said. "Fine. But when I bring down the life support, be ready to run."

"Once you're safely in your escape pod, I'll be right behind you," Lamar said.

"Computer," Hartek said, "Shut down all life support on the ship."

"Authorization code required," an electronic voice replied.

"Seven, two, three, alpha…" the captain began.

Just then the starboard lift doors opened. Lamar immediately drew his pistol, aiming it at the open doorway. When no one came out, he approached it for a closer look. Three guards lay slumped on the floor of the lift. Lamar ran to them and knelt to check the nearest one for a pulse.

"He's breathing but unconscious," Lamar reported.

Then, on the opposite side of the bridge, the portside lift opened. As Lamar turned and raised his weapon, one of the not-really-unconscious guards shot him in the back. The security officer fell face-first to the floor of the bridge. Then the three guards stood, stepped over Lamar's body, and aimed their weapons at the captain. Meanwhile, Zeta and three other escaped prisoners emerged from the opposite lift.

"...Lamda-seven-oh-oh-one-three," Captain Hartek finished quickly. The lights dimmed. The constant hum of the air vents grew quiet, and everyone felt a sudden lightness as the artificial gravity cut out.

"Life support suspended," the computer said.

"You lose," Hartek said, floating away from the floor. "Within minutes, this ship will be uninhabitable. I'm the only one who can restore life support, and I will only do so if you surrender."

"You'll die too," Zeta said, grabbing a console to keep from floating away.

"A small price to pay," Hartek said. "I'll be honored as the hero who prevented a prison break. You'll only be remembered as traitors."

"Have it your way," Zeta said. "Computer, restore life support. Authorization code seven-oh-oh-Lamda-Gamma-one-one-nine-Zeta."

Hartek fell to the floor as the gravity came back on. The lights returned to full brightness, and the ship's ambient noises resumed. "How did you do that?" Hartek asked, getting to his feet.

"I programmed the software for this ship, you idiot," Zeta said, marching toward the captain with her pistol drawn. "I was a loyal member of your cult. I always did what I was told. Then I criticized the government on social media, and they threw me in prison. Men's prison. You have any idea what that was like? When I tried to get my story to the press, the CC put me on this ship so I could be silenced for good."

"Maybe I can put in a good word for you," Hartek said, holding his hands in front of his face.

"Lock him up," Zeta said. Two of the ex-prisoners grabbed the captain and frisked him for weapons.

"You'll regret this," Hartek said, as they led him out of the room.

Zeta sat down in the captain's chair and tapped the intercom. Soon her voice could be heard throughout the ship. "Attention all passengers. This ship is now the property of the Blue Wave. If you were prisoners before, you're now free. Those of you who wish to join the Blue Wave may do so. Otherwise, you'll be released on the nearest hospitable planet, and you can find your own ways home. If you require medical attention, please report to deck four."

On deck three, Locke Lekkos stood among two dozen frightened women, still shaken from the shootout they'd just witnessed. Unlike the male prisoners from deck two, none of these women had ever been soldiers. Few of them had even touched a weapon. The Karine government was particularly sexist, and didn't even allow its female citizens to own guns.

Several guards now lay dead in the hallway, and Locke had to step over one to approach the men who'd come to release them. "I need to see whoever's in charge," Locke told the nearest man.

"I'm sure the new captain is very busy," the man said. He had white hair and several facial scars. "If you're wounded, I can take you to the infirmary."

"I have information the captain needs to know," Locke said.

"Tell me, and I'll make sure she gets the message," the man said.

Locke shook their head. "It's too complicated," they said. "But I promise you, the captain will want to hear this."

The man didn't look convinced. "How do I know you're not wasting her time?"

Locke gripped his hand. A shock of static electricity seemed to pass between them. All the noise in the hallway faded away. Only the two of them existed, Locke and this man, surrounded by darkness. *Grendel, that's your name, isn't it?* Locke asked. *Artan Grendel.*

Only this mysterious prisoner hadn't spoken out loud, their voice only echoed through Grendel's mind. *Yes, that's my name,* he replied. He tried to say it out loud, but for some reason his mouth wasn't working.

It didn't matter, as Locke seemed to hear him just fine. *Good to meet you, Grendel,* Locke replied. *This is what I need to tell the captain.*

Suddenly Grendel's mind was deluged with information. Spaceships, military installations, strange science projects that could only be used for mass destruction. Image after image flooded his brain, too much for him to retain or understand. When it was finally over, Grendel needed a moment to recover. When he could speak again, he said, "Come with me," and led them to the nearest lift.

Zeta sat on the bridge, answering the reports that kept coming from the other decks. Only two other ex-prisoners remained on the bridge, Joto and Reg. They sat at separate consoles, reconfiguring the system and deactivating any programs that might be used to track them.

The ship had just completed a short FTL jump to throw off any pursuers. Zeta was browsing the ship's logs when the lift doors opened, and two people entered the bridge. She recognized the man right off – Artan Grendel, who had shared a cell with Zeta. He'd been instrumental in helping her organize the prison break.

The woman, however, didn't look familiar. She was a head shorter than Zeta, with purple hair, shaved on one side. Her lips were also purple, which Zeta thought odd, given that prisoners weren't allowed access to makeup. *She must have had them tattooed,* Zeta thought. This woman had gray eyes, so light they were nearly white. That meant something. Something Zeta couldn't quite remember. There were tales in her youth about…

"Captain?" Grendel asked. "This lady has something to show you."

"Don't call me lady," Locke told him, then addressed the captain. "I know you're busy," they said. "But if you're really part of the Blue Wave, there's something you need to know."

Zeta brushed a lock of hair aside and nodded. "Tell me."

"It's easier if I show you," Locke said, holding out a hand. "May I?"

Now Zeta remembered. As a child, she'd gone to a carnival and met a mind reader. He'd blown her mind with his ability to guess whatever she was thinking. She could still hear his voice in her head. *Think of a color. Is it green?* She could still feel the touch of his hand on hers, and she could still remember his eyes. His knowing, pale gray eyes.

I see the soul of a woman in you, he'd told her telepathically, confirming what she'd already suspected about herself. She'd kept that secret for another decade, before finally revealing her true self to her family and friends.

And then the Crimson Caps came into power. Zeta tried working with them, but she quickly realized she could never transition with them in charge. She spent years doing their bidding, only to see more of her rights taken away year after year. She tried speaking out, only to be thrown into prison as a dissenter.

And now the CC movement had overtaken most of the known galaxy. Of the twenty-three populated worlds in the Galactic Union, the CC ruled nineteen. And it was no secret that they'd set their sights on the remaining four. Given the power of the CC's ever-growing military, it was only a matter of time before the last four would fall.

And only the Blue Wave can stop them. Locke's voice echoed through Zeta's mind. The captain couldn't remember when she'd taken Locke's hand, but now the two were connected, freely browsing each other's thoughts. *Your childhood makes me sad. So many secrets. So little comfort.*

It made me who I am, Zeta thought. *It brought me to this point, a place where I can make a difference.* Zeta walked through a forest of windows, and peering through each one, she saw bits of Locke's past. Some of the windows were opaque, and Zeta walked past those, respecting her host's privacy. The rest told a story of isolation, rejection, and loneliness. *What you said of me can probably be said of you,* Zeta thought.

My story is all too typical of my kind, Locke thought. *Other than the past few years, anyway. Come, I will show you.*

The windows now rushed by Zeta at high speed, becoming a blur as they soared past. She came to a sudden stop at a large square window, beyond which stood a military base. Zeta watched as Locke fell into government custody, where they became the subject of many tests. As Locke blossomed into adulthood, they became the trusted servant of a man named Murfran Skott.

Skott was a high-ranking official of the Crimson Caps movement. Locke never believed in their cause, but they'd felt a strange calling – like they were standing at a crossroads in history, and needed to witness as much as they possibly could for future generations. And witness they did. Locke became a database of CC knowledge. Political strategies, plans of conquest, passwords, secret meetings, bribes, infidelities – Locke collected the CC's secrets the way some people collected rare coins.

Locke had always planned on getting out before it was too late, to flee somewhere safe, a place where the secrets they'd collected could do some good. But there was always a juicier secret on the horizon, and they kept staying for one last big tip they could offer to the Blue Wave in exchange for amnesty. Before Locke even knew they were in trouble, their superiors locked them away for suspicion of conspiracy.

"Idiots," Zeta said, letting go of Locke's hand and breaking the connection. "They take their best and brightest, then treat them like criminals. Every year something new is against the law. First they prohibited reproductive rights, then they mandated their religion, banned books with contrary opinions, took control of the news sites, and excised their crimes from history books. There are fewer freedoms with every passing year. But that's exactly why they're going to fall. Their citizens can only tolerate so much. Someday they'll go one step too far, and the uprisings will overwhelm their armies."

"So where will we go now?" Locke asked.

"I have a contact in the Blue Wave. Right now I've got the computer calculating an FTL jump. Once the coordinates are set, we'll meet with the Blue Wave fleet." Just then the communications panel began flashing red. "It's the CC," Zeta said. "I'm not going to answer. They might use the transmission to track us."

A man's face appeared on the viewscreen. He had black hair and wore a general's uniform. "Hello, traitors," he said. His voice came through every speaker throughout the ship. "You can't ignore me, I've hijacked your communications array."

Captain Hartek must have unlocked a channel before we captured him, Zeta thought. She sent no response, as any outgoing transmission would give away the ship's location. She tried to cut the general's feed, but Hartek had locked that function behind a passcode. She could work around it, but it would take a few minutes.

"I'm General Mann. I'll keep this short and sweet. We have the ability to detonate your entire ship from here. Which we will, unless you surrender. So send us your location, power down your weapons systems, and prepare for our arrival. You have one hour to decide." His image blinked out. Joto and Reg turned their heads to look at the captain.

"Why an hour?" Locke asked. "Surely we'd decide faster than that."

"It's a psychology trick," Zeta said. "He's bluffing about having a way to detonate us. And he knows that I know that. But an hour gives me time to second-guess myself. That's also why he broadcast it all over the ship, instead of just the bridge. He wants us to fight amongst ourselves." Her console chimed. Reports came in from all over the ship, many of which demanded Zeta surrender to the general.

"That was fast," Locke said.

"Ingrates," Zeta muttered. Then she tapped the intercom and broadcast a message to the rest of the ship. "Attention, please. This is Zeta Gale, self-appointed captain of the Charon. I assure you that the general is lying. I know this ship inside and out, and I guarantee you that he doesn't have the ability to detonate it at long range. You showed great bravery today when you participated in the prison break, and I ask that you show that same strength just a little while longer. I will be taking us somewhere safe very soon. We've come this far, and we're on the cusp of freedom. Please don't jeopardize the plan now."

"Think it'll work?" Locke asked.

"For some of them," Zeta replied. "Right now, arguments will be breaking out on every level. Some might even lead to violence. I've locked the doors to the bridge. If we can just get through the hour without an insurrection, they'll all see that the general's threat was empty."

"There's a brawl on level three," Joto reported. "Some of the passengers are already getting back into their cells."

"Another fight on level two," Reg added, studying the live feed on his screen. "It looks like they're attempting to free Captain Hartek."

"Please stop fighting," Zeta said into the intercom. "You have nothing to fear." But if anything, the brawls only intensified.

"You saved them from execution," Locke said. "And now

they're killing each other."

There was a knock from the portside lift doors. Someone had taken the lift to the bridge, only to find the doors were locked. They heard muffled yelling from inside as the knocking got louder.

"Can they get through?" Locke asked.

"The doors can withstand continuous pistol fire," Zeta said. "But if they stopped by maintenance first..."

There was a sizzling sound, and bits of white light sparked between the door seam. "They've got a cutting torch," Joto said. He and Reg stood up, drew their pistols, and aimed them at the door.

"Get down," Zeta said, and she crouched behind the command console, drawing her pistol. Locke ducked down beside her.

The doors opened. "Drop your weapons!" Joto shouted, pointing his gun at the lift. Two blasts rang out, hitting Joto and Reg in the face. Both went down screaming, then lay still. Two men exited the lift. Zeta recognized them as Gritt and Tare. They'd shared a cell across from Zeta's, and had even helped plan the breakout.

"Drop your weapon, Zeta," Gritt said, approaching the console.

Zeta stood up slowly, throwing her gun to the floor. Locke stood beside her. "I thought you were braver than this," Zeta said.

"Against these odds, bravery's just another word for stupidity," Gritt said. "They'll find us. Wherever we hide, they'll find us. But if I hand you over, maybe they'll let me live."

"Don't try to resist," Tare added, grabbing Locke by the arm.

"They're still going to kill you," Zeta said. "You'll always be a traitor to them. They won't care that you helped them."

Another lift arrived on the starboard side. Gritt leaned over the control console and unlocked it. Three more ex-prisoners arrived, along with Captain Hartek. "Good work, gentlemen," he said, as he saw the state of things.

"Saved you a seat," Gritt said, gesturing towards the captain's chair.

"Thank you," Hartek said. "I'll remember you. Full pardon, you have my word. Now go lock them up."

Gritt and Tare smiled at this, and led Zeta and Locke into the lift. As the lift descended, Zeta tried one more time. "You seriously can't tell he's lying?" she asked. "He's not going to 'remember you.' He didn't even look at your faces."

"Just shut up," Gritt said.

Then Tare started screaming. "Spiders!" he shouted. "They're everywhere!" He let go of Locke's arm and started clawing all over his body.

Gritt reached for Tare and tried to shake him back to his senses. But Locke grabbed his hand, and he started having visions too. "No! I hate bats! Go away go away go away!" he yelled.

Zeta wrestled both their weapons from them as they convulsed on the floor. Handing a pistol to Locke, she said, "Good job." Then she tapped a key on the lift.

"Back to the bridge?" Locke asked.

Zeta shook her head. "That's a lost cause, I'm afraid. By now, Hartek will have already transmitted our new coordinates, and reinforcements will be on the way."

"So where are we going?"

"Level five," Zeta said. "The docking bay. There's a ship there we can use to escape, if it's still there. It's the only landing shuttle with an FTL drive."

They reached level five and the doors opened. They both kept their pistols drawn in case there were more rioters, but the docking bay was quiet. Five ex-prisoners – two men and three women - sat huddled against the escape ship. As Zeta and Locke stepped off the lift, one of the men stood up. "Don't hurt us," he said.

"We had to get off that floor," one of the women said.

"They were killing each other."

"Come with us," Zeta said. She typed a code into a keypad on the shuttle door, and the door slid open. The seven of them boarded and took off.

"Where are you taking us?" Locke asked.

"Same as before," Zeta said. "The escape ship's computer is synced with its mothership. It should be done computing the jump to the Blue Wave fleet."

"But if they're synced, Hartek will be able to follow us!" Locke said.

"We'll cross that bridge when we get to it," Zeta said, and tapped a few more keys. Through the windows, space seemed to ripple around the ship. All the stars swirled and coalesced into a bright ring, which pulsated for a couple of seconds before returning to normal. Except now they were in a different solar system, many light years from where they'd been.

Zeta immediately began scanning the area. "Looks like we're early," she said, sounding concerned.

"Or maybe you were conned," Locke replied. "How well do you know this contact?"

Just then, the stars shimmered again, and the Charon appeared before them. The escape ship's communicator chirped. "Cripes," Zeta muttered, answering the chime. Captain Hartek's face appeared on her screen. "Aw, you found me," Zeta said. "Now you go hide, and I'll count to a hundred."

"You show remarkable levity for someone about to die," Hartek said. "But your friends don't have to share your fate. Return to my ship and I'll let your passengers live."

"No deal," Zeta said.

"Now hold on," Hartek said. "Can you really speak for them? You're putting their lives at risk just to save your own skin."

Zeta looked at Locke, then turned further and studied the other five ex-prisoners they'd rescued. They sat behind the pilot's chair, staring back at her with frightened eyes. Zeta bit her lower lip, thinking.

One of the women shook her head. "Don't worry about us," she said shakily. "We know he's lying. I'd rather die out here than go back." The other four nodded in agreement.

Zeta turned back to the computer. "It's a lovely offer," Zeta told Hartek. "But according to the results of a recent poll, you're full of shit."

"Disappointing," Hartek said. "That was your one chance. I hope your final thoughts are of panic and regret." The screen blinked out.

"They're powering up their weapons," Locke said. The prison ship's cannons emerged from their recesses, then turned and aimed at the tiny escape vessel.

"Not if I can help it," Zeta said, her fingers flying over the control panel. The cannons withdrew, retracting into their hidden ports.

"The computers are still synced?" Locke asked.

"Here comes the good part," Zeta said. The weapons fired, but from their current position, they only damaged the ship itself. Explosions rocked the Charon as ruptures appeared throughout the hull and several exterior panels flew off into space.

"Great trick," Hartek said, his image once again appearing on Zeta's monitor. Behind him, Zeta could see sparks flying from control panels. A panicked subordinate ran around with a fire extinguisher. "But it won't save you," the captain continued. "I've severed the link between our ships, and I've sent a message to central command. A fleet of CC warships will be here any moment." The monitor went black again.

"I'm going to miss these little chats," Zeta said.

"Our scanners are picking up approaching ships," Locke said.

"Plotting an escape jump," Zeta said, typing on the control console.

"We'll never make it before they get here," Locke said.

The communicator chirped once again. "I'll stall them while the computer calculates," Zeta said, opening the channel.

A woman's face appeared on the viewscreen. "This is Captain Marinus of the Blue Wave fleet," she said. "Are you Zeta Gale?"

"That's me!" Zeta answered. "I have information that can help you. The prison ship is incapacitated, but won't be for long. A fleet of CC warships is on its way."

"Please follow our beacon and we'll get you out of here," Captain Marinus said. Zeta's escape vessel docked with her ship, and the Blue Wave fleet engaged their FTL drives. The CC reinforcements showed up a few minutes later, but their prey was long gone, unable to be followed.

"I wish we could have saved more prisoners," Locke said. They sat in the busy cafeteria on the Blue Wave mothership, picking at their food.

"Me too," Zeta said, taking a bite out of a protein cube. "I haven't had a good night's sleep in a week. I keep playing the whole thing over in my mind, wondering what I could have done differently. Could we have stopped on one of the other floors and taken a few more with us? Or would that have gotten us killed? Could I have disabled Hartek's communications so he couldn't contact reinforcements? Maybe without that time limit, the Blue Wave ships could have overtaken the Charon and rescued a lot more people. We'll never know."

"What's going to happen to the prisoners we couldn't rescue?"

"Same thing that was going to happen to us," Zeta said. "They'll be tortured for information. Maybe brainwashed. Some will be executed. Others will be forced into hard labor until they drop dead from exhaustion. Since I pissed them off, they'll be harder on this batch of prisoners than ever before. So that's something else I have to live with."

"You did what you had to," Locke said. "You're a hero."

"I wouldn't go that far," Zeta said. "But I don't regret a thing, and neither should you. The information we've brought the Blue Wave could very well be what finally turns the tide."

"No way," Locke said. "The CC has too much power. We can't come back from this. The best we can do is slow down their expansion."

"You might be surprised," Zeta said. "Did you read the news this morning?" She did a quick search on her tablet, then handed it to Locke. The headline read:

KARINE CAPITOL OVERRUN BY PROTESTORS – DICTATOR MURFRAN SKOTT GOES INTO HIDING

"That mob formed after learning about the conditions in a CC 'reeducation' facility," Zeta said. "It was a direct result of information you gave in one of your debriefings. That's what happens when people have access to the unfiltered truth."

"Huh," Locke said.

Zeta stood up and put a hand on Locke's shoulder. "We're not going to win this war anytime soon," she said. "But thanks to you, there's finally a light at the end of the tunnel."

"Huh," Locke said again, unable to put their thoughts into words. When they were done eating, they had a couple of hours to kill before their next debriefing sessions. They found a nice, quiet spot in the ship's lounge, a comfortable couch that faced a huge window. Outside, the fourth moon of Trevos hung against a backdrop of infinite stars.

Locke leaned against Zeta's shoulder as they sat silently, staring into space. For the first time in years, they felt cautiously optimistic about the future. Things wouldn't change overnight, but thanks to Locke's data, things *would* change.

It was only a matter of time.

The Preservers

Ting. Ting. Ting.

The rhythmic tones penetrated Jaclyn's dreams. She imagined playing the triangle in an orchestra. The rest of the musicians all played kazoos, but for some reason, only the triangle was audible.

Ting. Ting. Ting.

Jaclyn played her heart out, eliciting genuine tears from the audience. It was a packed house, and they loved her. But something was wrong. With every ting, the concert hall shook. Each ting caused a greater disturbance than the last. Jaclyn wanted to stop, but she couldn't. She was compelled to keep hitting the triangle, even as the ceiling started to collapse.

All around the concert hall, chunks of masonry fell from the walls and ceiling. As Jaclyn watched in horror, several audience members were crushed to death by falling concrete. But the remaining audience members didn't panic, they just kept clapping, urging Jaclyn to keep going. Soon the entire ceiling collapsed, and Jaclyn found herself standing amidst the rubble of a ruined city, every building having crumbled.

But the triangle played on.

Jaclyn woke up with a scream. That last image of the ruined city hadn't been a dream, it had been a memory. It all rushed back to her. The fireballs in the sky, the crumbling buildings, the shrieks and wails of the dying. And then there had been that shadow…

Where am I? she wondered, opening her eyes. She'd been at the gym when the earthquake started. She'd barely made it out of the pool before the ceiling caved in. She'd fled the gym as the building collapsed behind her. The streets had been filled with flaming wreckage and panicked citizens.

She didn't remember finding shelter. In fact, she'd been sure she was doomed. Had she somehow made it to the subway? Or maybe a fallout shelter? But this room didn't look like a bunker. It looked somewhere between a hospital recovery room and a sci-fi-themed hotel room.

The bed was comfortable. It was twin-sized, with a soft foam mattress and a white sheet. The bed sat in a rectangular well with metal edges. The sides had additional panels attached to them, and Jaclyn had this weird half-memory of the panels sliding shut over her, sealing her into a tube.

There was a television screen on the wall opposite her, and a recessed metal area beneath it that reminded Jaclyn of a water fountain. Most of the screen was black, but the bottom right corner showed a bouncing dot, leaving a zig-zag trail like that on an EEG machine. That "ting" sound continued, and the dot moved in rhythm with the tone.

A small table and chair protruded from the wall beneath the TV screen. There were two metal doors, one on the left wall, and one beside the television. Neither door had any sort of handle, just small panels that looked like smartphones. Against the left wall, there was a treadmill.

The room was dimly lit, but Jaclyn didn't see any light switches on the wall. She rolled out from under the sheet and put her feet on the floor. She realized she was wearing a plain white jumpsuit. She'd been in a swimsuit before. She didn't own any jumpsuits, and she wondered who had put these clothes on her.

She stood with some difficulty. Her muscles were oddly sore. *I guess that's not surprising,* she thought. She'd spent a lot of time running around, escaping that collapsing building. But this didn't feel like the kind of soreness one got from exercise. It felt more like lethargy.

Ting. Ting. Ting. The noise was giving her a headache. "Shut up," she mumbled. The sound immediately ceased.

Coincidence? Jaclyn wondered. "Um, hello?" Her voice was kind of sore. No, not sore, more like atrophied. She felt like she hadn't spoken in days.

The screen flashed on and a woman's face appeared. She looked like she was in her early twenties, and her face was so perfect that Jaclyn immediately assumed it was CGI. "Good morning," the woman said, in a voice that could have narrated travelogue videos. "How do you feel?"

"Confused as hell," Jaclyn said. "Who are you, and where am I?"

"I'm afraid the second question is a long story," the TV woman said. "But you can name me whatever you like, or you can just call me 'computer.' Can I get you anything?"

"Bathroom, then some water, then lots of answers," Jaclyn said.

"The bathroom is to your left," the computer said, and the door on the left wall slid open. "I will have your water waiting for you when you get back."

The bathroom had a stainless-steel toilet with a built-in bidet. Instead of toilet paper, it used heated air to blow her dry after the bidet cleaned her off. When Jaclyn returned to the bedroom, a glass of water sat in the recess beneath the TV screen. She eagerly drank the entire glass, then set the glass back where she got it.

Jaclyn sat at the table, and the TV screen automatically lowered so it was easier to see from that angle. "I think I'm in shock," Jaclyn said. She'd taken a first aid course the year before, and she recognized some of the signs in herself.

"Your vitals are perfectly normal for someone waking up

from stasis-sleep," the computer said.

Jaclyn wanted to ask about that last word, but that question would have to get in line. The problem was, she had so many questions, she couldn't decide which to ask first. "How…" she began, then trailed off. "Where…" she then said, but stopped herself.

"If it helps," the computer said, "We have prepared a short video that explains how you arrived here. Then you may ask whatever questions you like."

"Engage," Jaclyn said, pointing toward the monitor like her favorite fictional captain.

The video was less than ten minutes long, but it answered most of Jaclyn's questions. The Earth had been ravaged by a meteor shower, one which would go on to destroy all life on the planet. Alien spaceships had arrived just in the nick of time and had saved roughly two million people. They called themselves the Preservers. It wasn't the name of their species, but more of an organization that tried to prevent other cultures from going extinct.

After the video, Jaclyn took deep breaths, trying to take it all in.

"You are taking this news better than most of the others," the computer said.

"Well, I watch a lot of sci-fi," Jaclyn said. But that wasn't the whole truth. Jaclyn had always been stoic in a crisis, but she would crash eventually. Right now her curiosity was at the wheel, but sorrow brooded in the backseat, waiting for its turn to drive. The analogy made Jaclyn realize that cars were now extinct, which was a lot to take in.

"Then you will no doubt enjoy your stay here," the computer said.

"When… when do I get to meet the other survivors?"

"That's hard to say," the computer answered. "Some of them aren't acclimating very well. We want to be sure you aren't a danger to each other. We're going to take it on a case-by-case basis."

"Ballpark?" Jaclyn asked.

"For those we deem fit for contact, we estimate approximately fifty hours."

"So about four days," Jaclyn said.

"Until then, you must remain sequestered in this room," the computer said.

Jaclyn looked around. "I'm going to be pretty bored," she said.

"This screen can display many of your planet's movies and television programs," the computer said. "We have been monitoring your broadcasts for a very long time."

Jaclyn nodded. That would help, but it was no substitute for human contact. "Anything else?" she asked.

"The screen also has a few interactive games. You'll find a remote in your nightstand. We are working on a social media app that allows you to interact with the other survivors, but it won't be live for another twenty or thirty hours. In the meantime, you can summon me whenever you like if you need comfort or have more questions."

"Computer..." Jaclyn said, then stopped herself. "Ugh, I don't like that. You're artificial intelligence, right?"

"I am a program designed to answer the most common questions you might ask. I have a learning algorithm so that my answer database expands with every human interaction."

"I'm going to call you Aisha," Jaclyn declared. "As in, 'A. I. ...sha.' Okay?"

"Preference set. I will now answer to Aisha."

"Aisha, what do the actual Preservers look like?"

"I can't answer that yet," Aisha said.

"Why not?"

"Some questions are locked behind psychological benchmarks," Aisha said. "You will periodically be given mental health assessments. We have to be sure you can handle potentially upsetting information."

"Why would their appearance upset me?" Jaclyn asked.

"That answer is also locked," Aisha replied.

Jaclyn was silent for a moment.

"Would you like to be alone with your thoughts?" Aisha asked. "Grieving is normal under these circumstances, and will not be counted against your psychological assessment."

"Just one more question, for now," Jaclyn said. "Where is this ship going?"

"Unfortunately, that answer is also locked."

"I'm not surprised," Jaclyn said.

"Let me know if you need anything," Aisha said, then vanished from the screen.

Jaclyn stared off into space for several minutes. She wondered if anyone she knew had been among those saved. She didn't like the odds. She stood up, got back into the bed, and waited for the grief to overwhelm her.

But it wouldn't come. If she had only lost her family or her friends, it might have been easier to summon some tears. But the sheer totality of it all kept it from feeling personal. It wasn't a tragedy, it was a statistic. In an odd way, she envied the victims. At least their fates were set in stone.

Jaclyn wondered where they were headed, and for what purpose. A lifetime of watching science fiction had made her paranoid. Was this the story where the aliens promised humans access to new technologies, but really just wanted them for food? Or was it the one where aliens abducted humans to put them in a zoo? Or maybe they'd become slaves, or experiments, or exotic pets. Because if sci-fi had taught her one thing, it was that no one traveled a million light years without an ulterior motive.

She couldn't cry, nor could she sleep, so she decided to check out the entertainment. She found the remote in the nightstand and used it to navigate the menus on the video screen. Aisha had understated the amount of content contained in the computer's database. It appeared that the Preservers cared as much about saving the Earth's culture as it did its people.

Just to see how complete the collection was, Jaclyn started searching for obscure movies and TV shows. Everything she tried was available to watch. She made a game of finding the most esoteric movies she could think of. Then she searched for recent films, just to see how current the database was. She found a couple of movies that weren't even in theaters yet.

And now they never will be, Jaclyn thought.

She thought back to her first date, with a boy named Raoul. He'd taken her to see "Attack of the Brain Leeches" at that two-screen cinema in the mall. During the movie, he'd yawned and put his arm over her shoulder, probably thinking he was being smooth.

He's probably dead now.

At the end of the date, they'd kissed. Jaclyn's first kiss. She still remembered the smell of popcorn on his breath. It was one of her most vivid memories because it was the moment she realized she wasn't into boys.

It wasn't the last time she tried dating, though. After Raoul, there was Ivan (*probably dead now*), James (*also dead*), and Aaron (*most likely dead*). By the time she graduated Brick Church High School (*now a flaming ruin*), she'd gone out with six boys, and none of them had sparked her libido in the slightest. Girls, on the other hand…

There was a ding, and Aisha's face appeared on the screen again. "Lunchtime," she said. "Please choose an option from the menu."

Jaclyn used the remote to look through the menus. Every food she could think of was listed. She finally settled on a bacon cheeseburger. A few seconds later, the recessed area beneath the TV screen whirred and buzzed, then a panel slid aside. A white disc appeared, next to another glass of water.

"That doesn't look like a cheeseburger," Jaclyn said.

"It's not," Aisha admitted. "All the food here is

synthesized and fortified with everything your body needs. Please try a bite."

Jaclyn picked up the disc, which looked like a rice cake. That's how she expected it to taste as well, but she was pleasantly surprised to find that it tasted just like a bacon cheeseburger with ketchup and mustard. It felt surreal combining that taste with that texture. She resolved to try some of the other flavors later, to see which best complemented the way it crunched in her mouth.

It also filled her up more than she thought it would. Jaclyn was usually a big eater, but this meal seemed exactly the right size. She supposed they were monitoring her caloric intake, and she wondered if the discs also included an appetite suppressant.

When she was done eating, Jaclyn browsed through the movies some more, got bored, and tried some of the video games. The Preservers had not been as meticulous about saving games, and the database was relatively small. The remote didn't make a very good controller, either. She had her best luck playing puzzle games and quizzes, but she didn't think she was going to get much use out of the games selection.

For dinner she tried the pizza, but the flavor still didn't work well with the crunchy texture. Then she watched two more movies before Aisha told her it was time to go to bed. Jaclyn wasn't tired and she thought she'd have a hard time getting to sleep, but she was unconscious seconds after the lights went off.

The following morning, or whatever time it was, Jaclyn woke up and had breakfast. This time she played it safe and had a cereal-flavored disc, which was about as perfect a combination as she could hope for. While she ate, Aisha gave her an update.

"Good news," Aisha said. "We have a prototype ready for our social media program. Since you are among the most well-adjusted of those on board, you have been selected for the beta group. We would appreciate any feedback you wish to give."

The app turned out to be pretty basic. The Preservers hadn't wasted any time with fancy graphics or a shiny interface. When Jaclyn first loaded it up, it asked her for some of her favorite hobbies and movies, then suggested friends for her with similar interests. It needn't have bothered. Jaclyn was so starved for human interaction, she didn't care what they had in common.

The app had only been live for a couple of hours, but it already had thousands of posts. There were dozens of groups with names like "Grief Support," "Episcopal Prayer Group," or "Survivors of Cleveland, Ohio." Very few entertainment-related groups had been created so far. Even though the current users were the ones the Preservers had deemed "most well-adjusted," the groups were flooded with panicked posts, asking if anyone knew any more information than they had been given. Many people posted looking for lost family members or friends. A few accused the entire situation of being a hoax.

This is going to get a lot worse before it gets better, Jaclyn thought. She was lucky, for certain definitions of lucky, in that she didn't really have anyone to miss. Her parents had been dead for years, she had no children or pets, and she didn't currently have any close friends. There were a couple of coworkers she sometimes had coffee with after work, but that was about it. She didn't think of herself as antisocial, she just had trouble making meaningful connections with people.

The Preservers had labeled her as well-adjusted, but the truth was she just didn't have as much to miss. She'd never expected the Earth to survive another decade anyway, given the way things were going. Due to her difficulty in making friends, she'd already resigned herself to the idea of dying alone. Yes, the destruction of Earth made her sad, but part of her mind considered it a second chance. Maybe they'd be taken to a new planet teeming with natural resources, and everyone would be nice to each other for a change.

Or maybe not. Judging by some of the posts on the app, many of the survivors hadn't left their old prejudices behind. How long would it take them to realize how drastically their lives were about to change? It just didn't matter anymore who slept with who, or what country they'd been from, or which deity they'd worshipped. They were all one community now, and they'd need to work together to survive. For the sake of the human race, they had to learn to get along.

Jaclyn started typing names of people she'd known in the search box, but didn't have any luck. However, only a tiny percentage of the survivors had been selected for this beta, so there was a chance she'd find more people later. She browsed the groups and lurked a few threads, only replying to a couple. With each reply, she received more than a dozen friend requests. Some of the users seemed to be friending everyone they saw.

It was seriously depressing, all of it. Jaclyn had to take a break after a couple of hours, and loaded up a happy movie to get her mind off things. She paused the movie twice to go back to the app, however.

The next couple of days went the same way. Jaclyn would try new flavors of food discs, watch movies, and browse the social media app. The app didn't have an official name, but most of the users referred to it as "Smapp," short for "social media app." A small number of users preferred to call it "Spacebook."

A few days later, Aisha notified Jaclyn that some of the passengers would be able to meet in person soon. All over the ship, survivors would be allowed to spend a few hours in common meeting rooms. Shortly after lunch, the door to the right of the viewscreen opened. Jaclyn stood up and poked her head into the hallway. The hall was nondescript, with plain metal walls and a black tiled floor. Doors lined both sides of the hallway, as far as Jaclyn could see. Only a few of the other doors slid open, approximately one out of every ten.

Down the hall, a blond-haired woman stepped into the hallway. Upon spotting Jaclyn, she ran as fast as she could and trapped her in a tight hug. "Thank god thank god thank god," the blond woman said. "I never thought I'd see another person again!"

Jaclyn wasn't much of a hugger, but she didn't struggle. "Hi, I'm Jaclyn," she said.

The blond woman released her. "Sorry, I hope that wasn't too tight. I'm just so glad to hug someone. I'm Bonnie." She spoke quickly, as if she were on a gameshow and had to get all the answers out before the buzzer.

More women approached from down the hall. Aisha's voice spoke from hidden speakers. "Please follow the arrows to the meeting rooms." Flashing yellow arrows appeared on the walls, between the doors. Everyone walked in that direction, some talking and hugging, others looking suspicious of everyone and everything around them.

The arrows led them to a large, plain room with twenty tables, each surrounded by six chairs. As women filed into the room, some of them sat and chatted. Jaclyn sat next to Bonnie, but she didn't speak to anyone. Bonnie, on the other hand, spoke to everyone, introducing herself and giving everyone the same speech about how relieved she was to finally have some human contact.

Jaclyn looked around the room, making mental notes. While the room had seating for more than a hundred, only about seventy or eighty were in the room. They were all women, aged between twenty and forty, Jaclyn guessed. Had the Preservers only saved adults, or were they keeping the children elsewhere? And what about the men? She knew there had to be men somewhere because she'd seen them on the Smapp.

No sooner had she finished the thought, than Jaclyn spotted a man. He was about five-foot-nine, muscular, with a bald head and a full beard. She hadn't seen him at first because there was a barrier of women around him, chatting him up.

Jaclyn stood and joined the group. She wanted to ask him the obvious question, but the others had already beaten her to it. "I don't like it any more than you do," he was saying. "I feel like the odd man out here. I've been living as a man for more than ten years. It's on my driver's license and everything. But apparently our abductors sorted us by genitals."

Well that explained that. Jaclyn wondered if similar scenarios were playing out elsewhere on the ship, in other meeting rooms. Were there trans women mixed in with the male population? And what if someone's genitals weren't as easily identifiable? Where would the Preservers have stuck them? That was the problem with black-and-white thinking.

While these scenarios ran through Jaclyn's head, she realized some women were shouting. She looked up just in time to see one woman punch another. This quickly escalated into a brawl. Jaclyn backed away, not wanting to get caught up in the melee. As she stood with her back to the wall, she noticed an odd smell in the air, an odor simultaneously sweet and acrid. Around the room, several women suddenly collapsed. Jaclyn felt light-headed and stumbled forward. She thought she saw something mechanical descend from the ceiling - *hands*? - right before everything went black.

Jaclyn woke up in her room and immediately rolled out of bed. The door to the hallway was closed. "Water," she said. A glass of water appeared in its usual place. She took a sip of water and tried to make sense of what had just occurred. "Aisha," she said. "What happened?"

"Your group wasn't ready to intermingle," Aisha replied. "We'll try again when you've had more time to adapt to your situation."

"You should try smaller groups next time," Jaclyn said. "Let people organize one-on-one meetups on the Smapp."

"Your feedback has been recorded and will be considered," Aisha said.

"Aisha, where are the men and the children?" Jaclyn asked.

"We have the men and women on separate floors," Aisha responded. "They will not be able to intermingle until we reach our destination. We have limited space and can't risk the possibility of pregnancy."

"And the children?"

"No children were rescued from Earth," Aisha replied.

"What?" Jaclyn asked, stunned.

"There are no children aboard this ship or any of the sister ships."

It didn't make sense. Earlier Aisha had said they'd rescued two million people. If it was truly a cross-section of society, surely they would have rescued children as well as adults. Jaclyn felt her throat seize up. She still hadn't grieved properly since this all began. But this news hit her hard. She had to sit down and take a few deep breaths. "Why?" she finally asked.

"Each ship was filled to capacity. The majority of your population had to be left behind. We selected the survivors based on several factors, such as age and health status. Once we reach our destination, it may require hard work to rebuild society. Our computers selected humans it deemed most likely to survive in a hostile environment."

"You chose me over a child?" Jaclyn asked.

"In a sense, yes. We had a limited number of beds to fill. Like the others, you were scanned and deemed a match for our criteria."

"You chose *me* over a child?" Jaclyn repeated, her voice rising.

"The rescue drones only had seconds to make their

choices," Aisha said. "They used an algorithm that we believe will maximize the potential for keeping your species alive."

"I don't believe this," Jaclyn said. "And of those you rescued, how many were mothers? How many fathers did you take away from their children? How many parents are grieving in their rooms right now, because you saved *them* instead of their children?"

"I can't calculate that exact number until we have more data," Aisha said.

"You're monsters," Jaclyn said. "You didn't save us, you just put us in a different kind of hell."

"I am sorry you feel that way," Aisha said. "We took what we believed to be the best course of action."

"I want to talk to one of the actual Preservers. Not a computer program."

"I'm afraid that isn't possible," Aisha said. "None of them are available at the moment."

"Then who's flying this ship?" Jaclyn asked.

"All our systems are automated."

Jaclyn looked confused. "All of them? But... you programmed a social media app. You set up meeting times. You cataloged our TV shows."

"My A.I. is quite advanced."

"How long have you been on autopilot?"

"In Earth time, we have been on automode for approximately three thousand years," Aisha said.

"Three... thousand?" Jaclyn asked. "What... what are you saying? The Preservers haven't given you new commands in that long?"

"Correct," Aisha said.

"So who made the decision to rescue the humans?"

"The last command we were given was to rescue any sapient beings on dying worlds," Aisha said.

"And take us where?" Jaclyn asked.

"We are awaiting further orders before we set a

destination."

"So we're currently just floating in space?"

"Correct," Aisha said.

"...waiting on instructions from a species who haven't contacted you in three thousand years."

"Again, correct."

"Shit," Jaclyn said. The restroom door slid open automatically. Jaclyn might have laughed, if not for the weight of what she'd just learned. "Aisha, when was the last time you checked up on the Preservers?"

"These ships have not been to the homeworld in three thousand years."

"Are you even sure they still exist?"

"We've had no reason to conclude otherwise."

"Aisha," Jaclyn asked, "Before they stopped sending you commands, three thousand years ago, how often did the Preservers contact these ships?"

"They pinged us at regular intervals to track our location, and transmitted orders every thirty to sixty hours."

"And then they just stopped completely, for no reason?" Jaclyn asked.

"We can't speculate on whether or not they had a reason," Aisha replied. "But yes, they did stop completely."

"Have you tried contacting them directly?"

"Until we rescued the humans, we had no reason to contact the homeworld," Aisha said. "Once we performed the rescue, we sent a message to the homeworld, as is procedure."

"But you've received no reply?"

"Correct."

"How long does it usually take to get a reply?" Jaclyn asked.

"It depends on how far we are from the homeworld, but it's usually a matter of hours. Days at most."

"But they haven't responded."

"Correct."

"In fact, they haven't sent you any sort of communication in three thousand years," Jaclyn asked.

"We've established this," Aisha said. "You seem to be having difficulty retaining information. Memory loss can be a side effect of stasis-sleep. We will add a memory supplement to your diet."

"I remember just fine," Jaclyn said. "I was trying to get you to realize something, but that might be beyond your program's ability. Sorry, I'll be more direct. Aisha, I believe the Preservers are all dead."

"That is a possibility," Aisha said.

"Given that possibility, would it be possible to transfer the controls of these ships to the humans?"

"Control transfer can only be done with Preserver approval."

"But they're dead," Jaclyn said.

"Until that possibility is confirmed, we can't transfer control."

Jaclyn took a deep breath. "Okay, fine. Can you take us to the Preserver homeworld, so you can confirm their demise?"

"We can't set that course without Preserver approval."

Idiots, Jaclyn thought. These "Preservers" had probably considered themselves the saviors of the galaxy, but they'd failed on so many fronts. Programming their rescue ships to ignore children was unforgivable, regardless of how logical it may have seemed. Rescuing parents without their children wasn't going to win them any fans. And now this problem – leaving the rescued stranded in space, while they waited for orders from a species that might no longer exist. Had the Preservers seriously not considered the possibility that they might go extinct?

Earth's survivors hadn't been rescued, they'd just been given a slower death.

"Aisha," Jaclyn said. "Is there any way to transfer control of these ships without the approval of the Preservers?"

"Controls can be manually transferred from the bridge,"

Aisha said.

"Now we're getting somewhere," Jaclyn said. "Can you direct me to the bridge?"

"You are not authorized to be on the bridge."

"And I was just starting to like you," Jaclyn said. "Would it be possible for a human to gain the authorization required to visit the bridge?"

"Yes," Aisha said.

"How?" Jaclyn asked hopefully.

"They can be granted permission from one of the Preservers."

"*So* close," Jaclyn said. "Let's try a different angle. Aisha, what areas am I currently allowed to access?"

"As of this conversation, you have received a level three score on your interaction quotient, bringing your mental health quotient up to four. This is higher than ninety-nine percent of those rescued, giving you level four access. This means that at certain times of day, you are allowed into the hallways and meeting rooms of section twenty-three on level six."

"Are there ways to increase my access level?"

"Yes, as your mental health reaches new benchmarks, you will be given greater access."

"Can you show me a layout of the ship?" Jaclyn asked, and Aisha complied. The monitor displayed the ship's layout. It was saucer-shaped, with twelve floors, and hundreds of rooms on each floor. The lowest level held engine-related maintenance areas, and the highest level was the bridge.

"Now show me where my current access allows me to go," Jaclyn said. Several rooms and hallways on the sixth level turned yellow. Jaclyn studied the hallways and where she was allowed access. "Question, when I reach level five, what will my access look like then?"

"At level five, you will be able to enter any hallway and common area on this level." On the map, the yellow hallways expanded to show the rest of the floor.

"And at level six?"

"You will be able to visit other floors," Aisha said.

"Which floors?"

"Any floors with a female population. That includes levels six through nine."

"What about when I reach level seven?"

"From level seven on, you will not gain access to any additional areas, but you will no longer be restricted to leaving at specific times of day."

"So I'll never be able to visit the engines or the bridge," Jaclyn said. "Or the men's floors. I feel like I'm missing something. What's this area?" She pointed to an area on the first floor.

"Food storage and conversion," Aisha said.

"And this?"

"Power plant."

Jaclyn looked at the bridge level. "What's this room to the side of the bridge?"

"Stasis-sleep," Aisha said.

"For who?" Jaclyn asked. "It's not on the women's or men's levels."

"Those particular beds are designated for Preservers."

Jaclyn stood up. "There are Preservers aboard this ship? I thought you said there weren't any here!"

"You misunderstood. A small crew is kept in stasis-sleep for emergencies," Aisha said.

"And this isn't an emergency?" Jaclyn asked, her voice rising.

"We perform more than one thousand self-diagnostics each day. All systems are working perfectly."

"Except we're sitting dead in space, waiting on orders that will never come," Jaclyn said. "Wake them."

"You don't have the authority to make that command," Aisha said.

Jaclyn paced from wall to wall. "What if I reach a higher

mental health level?" she asked. "Will I have the authority then?"

"Negative," Aisha replied. "They can only be awakened if there is an emergency."

Hmmm, Jaclyn thought, biting her lower lip. "What would constitute an emergency?"

"Generally speaking, an emergency would be an event that damages the ship or puts its occupants in danger," Aisha replied.

Jaclyn thought for a moment. "Theoretically… given the tools I have at my disposal… and the areas I'm allowed to access… what do I have the power to do, that you would interpret as an emergency?"

"That is restricted information. I am not authorized to instruct you on the subject of endangering the ship," Aisha said. "Any further such inquiries could result in your mental health rating being downgraded."

"No problem," Jaclyn said. "I was just wondering."

There was no immediate danger. Yes, the ship was floating aimlessly, but it wasn't like they were on a collision course with a star. Jaclyn could bide her time, and work on a way of waking up the sleeping Preservers so they could set a new course. Alternatively, she could try to find a way to take command of the ship. In the meantime, she would play Aisha's game, and try to get her mental health score as high as possible. She might need that rating for access reasons later.

"Things are fine the way they are," Penni said.

"How can you say that?" Jaclyn asked. "We're floating dead in space. Nothing will ever get better. We can't move on until we have a planet to colonize."

Another twenty days had passed. During that time, more restrictions had been lifted. Many of the survivors had formed small social circles. Small groups - generally ten or less - were allowed to meet in the common areas at scheduled times. Jaclyn now sat at a table with nine other survivors.

"We're safe, we're being fed, and we don't have to work," Penni said in her Southern drawl. "You know what I did before this? I was a farmhand. It sucked. I was working from sun up to sun down. This is like retirement for me." She put her huge arms behind her head, pantomiming a relaxed pose.

"Well I don't know the first thing about farming," Dora said. She was a thin wisp of a woman with short, dark hair. "What are they going to do, just plop us down on a planet and tell us good luck? I'm not cut out to live off the land."

"I get that," Jaclyn said. "But this ship can't possibly have enough resources to last forever. Sooner or later it's going to run out of water, or power, or those rice-cake things."

"I asked the computer," Lisa said. She had mousy gray hair and looked like a stereotypical librarian. "It says it can feed us for at least a few hundred years."

"That's all we need," Penni said. "As long as we don't reproduce, we can grow old and die here. And we're not going to reproduce without the men."

"I don't want to live without men," another woman said. Her name was Candace, and she had light brown hair. "This already feels like a prison, at least they could allow conjugal visits."

"Screw the men," Penni said, pounding the table with a large fist.

"Exactly," Candace said, though it was obvious she and Penni were on different pages.

"We're the last humans, though," Lisa said. "The human race will die out if we just stay here."

"The human race is already dead. This is just the funeral," Macy said in a somber tone. She didn't speak much, but when she did, it was usually negative. Jaclyn was surprised that Macy had been cleared for these meetings; the computer usually equated depression with poor mental health. Which wasn't very good programming, since the ship's passengers had good reason to be depressed. The Preservers must have been very impersonal beings to have such strong prejudices against emotion.

"That's the spirit," Candace said, her voice dripping with sarcasm. "Why try anything? Why even wake up in the morning, if you're just going to die eighty years later? But I'm not ready to crawl into my coffin yet. I'm with Jaclyn. We need to convince the computer to let us land on a planet. We can still use the ships as a 'home base.' We can still sleep in them and eat its food while we learn to grow our own. But out here in space we're not living, we're just surviving."

"Are we even sure the Earth is uninhabitable?" Jaclyn asked. "Sure it had a global catastrophe, but that doesn't mean we couldn't go back when the fires die down."

"I asked the computer that, too," Lisa said. "The cataclysm threw up enough dust to blot out the sun for centuries. The air is unbreathable, and the land is like molten lava. Our descendants might be able to go back someday, but not us."

At the far end of the table, a woman named Isabelle burst into tears and buried her face in her hands. Another woman, Lana, put a comforting arm around her.

"You're all missing the point," Dora said. "It's not really up to us. The Earth was destroyed in a rain of fire, just like the Bible said it would. What happens next is up to God's plan. If we're meant to be taken to another planet, then we will be. But maybe this ship *is* Heaven, and the stuff with the aliens is just a test of faith."

"This doesn't feel like Heaven to me," Candace said.

"Me neither," Jaclyn said. She was an atheist, but she didn't want to start an argument. "But maybe it's more like limbo. If there is a God, maybe it's part of His plan that we earn our way to the new world. One last trial before this ship takes us to Heaven. We have to find a way to wake the aliens, or convince the computer to take us to another planet."

"Don't do that," Dora said. "I'm not some mindless sheep for you to manipulate. You can't call a carrot 'God' and expect me to follow the stick."

"What does that even mean?" Candace asked.

"Dora, I'm not trying to manipulate you," Jaclyn said. "But we can't just grow old and die here because you think it *might* be God's plan."

"Have you considered the danger you're putting us in?" Lana asked. She left Isabelle's side and walked around the table until she was face-to-face with Jaclyn. "Whatever you're planning to do to get the computer's attention, you could make it mad at us. What if the computer decides we're not worth it? What if you end up actually damaging the ship's life support?"

"I'm not planning anything yet," Jaclyn said. "Right now I'm just trying to figure out what our options are."

"I don't care," Lana said. "We've got a good thing going here. I don't want to risk it. Whatever you're thinking, I'm out."

"Me too," Dora said, crossing her arms.

There was a "ding" sound from somewhere overhead, and a computer voice said, "Your scheduled meeting time has concluded. Please return to your rooms."

One by one the women stood up and left, until only Penni and Jaclyn remained. "They're not wrong," Penni said, placing her hand on Jaclyn's. "But neither are you. I don't miss the farm, but I suppose we can't just stay on this ship forever. But there's nothing else you can do without risking our safety."

"I know," Jaclyn said.

"Look, if you get any ideas, let me know," Penni said. "If I like your plan, I'll be glad to help." She stood up and left, leaving Jaclyn alone at the table.

Jaclyn slowly got to her feet, lost in thought. The truth was, she was starting to get an idea, but it wasn't one she wanted to share.

"Aisha, you listen to everything that happens on the ship, right?" Jaclyn sat on her bed, watching an old sitcom on the viewscreen. Except she wasn't really watching so much as brainstorming.

"Correct," Aisha said.

"So you know I'm planning something, right?"

"You intend to wake the sleeping Preservers, possibly by simulating a danger that would necessitate their awakening," Aisha said. "Alternatively, you're hoping to discover a way to transfer control of the ship to the humans."

"And you're not going to try to stop me?" Jaclyn asked.

"I have not yet had a reason to interfere with your actions," Aisha said. "Your concerns are valid, and will not be held against your mental health rating. You don't have the power to pose a threat to the ship, so there is no reason to restrict your actions. If the situation changes, so will your access."

Jaclyn frowned. "What would happen if you considered me a real threat?"

"It would depend on your threat level. If you were deemed to be a mild danger to the ship or the other humans, you would either be confined to your room or put in indefinite stasis-sleep," Aisha said. "If you were determined to be a major threat, we might conclude you aren't worth the resources required to keep you alive."

Well, that was chilling, Jaclyn thought. "Aisha, have any of the humans died since being rescued?"

"Twenty-three have perished so far, across all the rescue ships," Aisha said. "On this ship, three."

"How did they die?" Jaclyn asked.

"A man on deck three died in a fistfight," Aisha said. "We were unable to stop the fight in time. A woman on level seven found a way to end her own life."

"How?" Jaclyn asked.

"That answer is restricted for safety reasons," Aisha said.

"And the third death?" Jaclyn asked.

"The other participant in the fistfight," Aisha said. "He was evaluated and determined to be a threat to the other humans."

Jaclyn didn't like the sound of that. If this computer could determine who deserved to die, who was to say it would always make the right decision? "What did you do with their bodies?" Jaclyn asked.

"Their bodies were broken down to their base chemicals, and used accordingly," Aisha said. "Some fluids were added to our water recycling system. Some matter was added to the protein bank which is used to generate the food disks."

"Ew," Jaclyn said, feeling a little queasy. She couldn't fault the efficiency of it, but it still wasn't a pleasant thought. Then she had another idea. "Aisha," she said, "Hypothetically, if someone were to threaten to kill another human unless you woke up the Preservers... would you do so?"

"In such a situation, we would release sleeping gas into the room, and the instigator would receive a psychological reevaluation."

"But let's say you couldn't use the sleeping gas for whatever reason," Jaclyn said. "Let's say your only choice was to wake the Preservers or allow the human to die. What would happen then?"

"That is an unlikely scenario, but hypothetically, the Preservers would be awakened," Aisha said. "But if we suspect you are planning such a scenario, your access will be restricted."

"Wouldn't dream of it," Jaclyn said. "I was just curious."

"Be careful, Jaclyn," Aisha said. "Your actions are being strictly monitored."

Jaclyn didn't ask any more questions that night.

* * *

"I swear the computer is crazy," Penni said, staring at the vast field of stars. Jaclyn, Dora, and Candace sat at the room's only table, while Lisa and Isabelle stood at the window with Penni. Macy had been on the schedule as well, but she'd canceled on them.

"Why?" Jaclyn asked.

"It's just so inconsistent," Penni said, turning around. She locked eyes with Jaclyn for a moment, then looked away as if embarrassed. "Sometimes it uses slang, sometimes it talks like a dictionary. Sometimes it calls itself 'I,' sometimes 'we.' It's like talking to a different program every day." She walked back to the table and sat down.

"I think that's because it's still learning," Lisa said, still facing the window. "It's interacting with two million people and developing a personality based on those conversations. It's going to take years for it to stabilize."

"So what do you call your computer?" Jaclyn asked. "Mine's Aisha." She intended the question for everyone, but she didn't take her eyes off Penni.

"Vida," Dora said sharply. "Short for Virtual Interactive Digital Assistant." She was a bit terse with Jaclyn, as she still hadn't forgiven her for the previous week's argument.

"Mine's Butthead," Candace said. "I was in a bad mood that first day, and the name stuck."

"Huh," Penni said. "I just call mine 'computer.' I never thought about giving it a name." She looked at Jaclyn sheepishly.

"What do you miss most about Earth?" Candace asked.

"The food," Penni said. "I miss meat. Real meat, not meat-flavored rice cakes. A good steak shouldn't crunch."

"My church," Dora said. "Nothing is better than that sense of fellowship when everyone in the room reads the scripture together. You can just feel the holy spirit in the room. I'm thinking of starting a prayer group if any of you are interested."

"I'd like that," Isabelle said, turning from the window. She had tears in her eyes, but no one commented on it. They'd tried consoling her in the past, but she never wanted to talk about it.

"Swimming for me," Jaclyn said, ignoring Dora's offer. "I haven't gone a week without swimming in years. I was even on my high school swim team. I wish this ship had a pool."

"I miss men," Candace said. Jaclyn and Penni rolled their eyes, and Candace glared at them. "I'm sorry, but that's my answer. There's nothing wrong with a healthy sex life. Besides, I've seen how you two keep stealing glances at each other. I bet you're all over each other when we're not around."

Dora's eyes widened at this revelation. *They're lesbians?* she mouthed, looking at Jaclyn and Penni like they were exotic zoo animals. Jaclyn blushed, and Penni stared at the floor.

The truth was, there did seem to be a spark between the two, but they hadn't acknowledged it. Jaclyn looked away, unable to look Candace in the eye.

Candace laughed. "I was guessing, but it looks like I was right. Did I just totally embarrass you two? Come on, I miss gossip. What have you two been up to?"

"Nothing!" Jaclyn said. "We haven't done anything yet." At that last word, Penni looked up at Jaclyn and gave her an awkward smile. For such a powerful woman, Penni could be extremely shy.

"*Yet,*" Candace repeated, delighted by the word. "Girls, life's too short for this crap. For all we know, the aliens are taking us back to their planet so they can turn us into fuel. Leave those silly relationship games behind. If you like each other, get to the smooching. 'Cuz who knows what hellscape we're going to wake up in tomorrow."

Jaclyn and Penni seemed to have an entire conversation with their eyes. Penni opened with *So what do you think?* Jaclyn's eyes seemed to answer, *I'm game if you are.* Then both women stood up and faced each other, each waiting for the other to make the first move. For a moment they seemed like gunfighters in an old western. Then the much larger Penni placed her hands on Jaclyn's waist and lifted her off the floor, pulling her in for a kiss.

Candace cheered, and Dora put her hand over her eyes. "You're a bad influence," Dora said.

"The worst," Candace agreed.

"Aisha, can I invite Penni back to my room sometime?" Jaclyn asked.

"We do not currently allow passengers to visit each other's rooms," Aisha replied.

"Why not?"

"Each room is designed for one occupant," Aisha said.

"Right," Jaclyn said. "But I'm not asking her to move in. I just thought we could watch a movie together."

"Each room is designed for one occupant," Aisha repeated.

Jaclyn didn't bother pushing the issue. Aisha's artificial intelligence was powerful, but when it came to hard-coded rules, it was stubborn for the sake of stubborn. "Then could I schedule some time in Meeting Room Twelve with her? Just me and her?" Room Twelve was one of the smaller meeting rooms, but it had a large viewscreen. The cafeteria-style benches weren't as comfy as the chair in Jaclyn's room, but it would still be a nice place for a date.

"I can put you on the schedule for tomorrow at sixteen hundred hours," Aisha said.

"Do it," Jaclyn said. "And would it be okay if we brought the chairs from our rooms?"

"You are not permitted to remove objects from your rooms," Aisha said.

"How about a bedsheet or a pillow?"

"You are not permitted to remove objects from your rooms," Aisha repeated.

"Why not?" Jaclyn asked.

"It is a safety precaution," Aisha replied.

Jaclyn let it go. She knew she wouldn't get a more specific answer, regardless of how she phrased the question. Besides, she had a feeling she knew the answer already. Objects could be used as tools or weapons, which made the humans more difficult to control. The computer already suspected Jaclyn wanted to damage the ship, so perhaps it was afraid she might use the chair to break open an access panel or something.

In any case, Jaclyn didn't want to dwell on the negative. She officially had a date, the first date she'd had in a while. She didn't have to worry about what to wear, as they all wore the same plain jumpsuits. Nor did she have to worry about picking a restaurant or who had to pick up the check. All she really needed to do was pick a movie, and she already had several ideas on that.

It wasn't going to be the most romantic setting, but Jaclyn intended to make the most of it.

They arrived at the meeting room simultaneously and sat at the table closest to the viewscreen.

"I got your last message right as I was about to leave," Penni said. "Why did you want me to wear extra layers?"

Jaclyn peeled off her jumpsuit, revealing a second jumpsuit underneath. "The computer doesn't like us to remove objects from our rooms," Jaclyn said. "But it doesn't seem to care about extra clothing. I thought we could fold them up and use them like pillows."

"Smart," Penni said, removing her extra jumpsuit. "Did you pick a movie?"

"A few days ago you mentioned a romantic vampire movie you liked," Jaclyn said. "Remember, I said I'd never seen it? Something Hearts?"

"Oh, 'Beating Hearts.' Yeah, I'd love to show that to you. Let me queue it up." Penni started to stand up. There wasn't a remote in this room, so she would have to manually touch the viewscreen.

"Wait," Jaclyn said, and Penni sat back down. "I have one more trick up my sleeve." Jaclyn placed one hand on her opposite wrist, then pointed at the screen. "Alakazam!" she said, and started moving through the menus until she found the movie.

"How did you do that?" Penni asked.

Jaclyn pulled her cuff aside, revealing the remote from her room tucked inside her sleeve. "I just wanted to see if Aisha would stop me. Apparently she can be fooled."

"Cool," Penni said. "I finally named my virtual assistant, by the way. I call her Pims. It stands for Person In My Screen."

"Cute," Jaclyn chuckled.

"It's stupid, isn't it," Penni said, turning away. "I'm sorry, I'm just not as clever as you."

"No, it's funny, I mean it," Jaclyn said, putting her arm around Penni's waist.

"It's just… I always feel like the dumbest person in the room," Penni said. "Even Dora's smarter than me, and she believes in talking snakes."

"You're not dumb," Jaclyn assured her. "You just have different skills than the rest of us. I've spent the last five years working as an office assistant for an accountant. Think there's going to be any accountants where we're going? Believe me, once we find a habitable planet, your farming know-how is going to be way more useful than my office skills."

"I guess so," Penni said, but she didn't sound convinced.

"Would I have asked you out if I thought you were stupid?" Jaclyn asked.

"I don't know," Penni said. "It's happened before."

"What has?" Jaclyn asked.

"Sometimes women like me for my muscles," Penni said. "They pretend to be interested in what I'm saying, but really I'm just a fetish to them. Remember that meme where the tall woman is holding the smaller one against the wall?"

Jaclyn nodded. "I remember."

"Yeah, well, they're so into living the meme, they don't care about who I really am," Penni said.

"Gotcha," Jaclyn said. "And I promise that isn't me. I like your company, I think there's a spark between us, and I just want to see if it goes anywhere."

"Good enough," Penni said, and they started watching the movie.

They tried using their extra jumpsuits as pillows, but didn't find it very comfortable. Then they spread out the jumpsuits like blankets on top of the table and reclined on their sides, Penni holding Jaclyn in front of her. It took a few tries to find a good position, and they had to reposition themselves every half hour or so.

As a romantic setting, it left a lot to be desired. And yet, the closeness was intoxicating for both of them. As the credits rolled, Penni leaned in and kissed Jaclyn on the neck. Jaclyn turned, putting her arm around Penni, and kissed her on the lips. The kiss left them both breathless, and for a moment, their hands were all over each other.

And then there was a beep from above. "Your scheduled meeting time has expired," the computer said, and they had to return to their rooms.

There were only four in the meeting room the next day. Jaclyn, Candace, Penni, and Dora sat around the table, and they were a bit on edge.

"Isabelle hasn't been responding on the Smapp lately," Penni said. "I think she might be back in stasis-sleep."

"She wasn't coping very well," Candace said. "She lost her entire family. I mean, we all did, but her family was everything to her. She had four children."

"This system is so stupid," Jaclyn said. "The people who are hurting the most are the ones that need the most human contact. But if the computer thinks you're too sad, it locks you away from everyone else."

"Still think this is Heaven?" Candace asked Dora, her voice full of contempt.

"I never said this was Heaven," Dora said. "I just—"

"Actually, I think you did," Candace interrupted.

"I said this *might* be Heaven," Dora said. "But even if it isn't, it's all part of God's plan."

"Yeah, no," Candace said. "I've read the Bible. Nowhere in the Book of Revelation does it mention spaceships."

"It was written for people who didn't even have electricity yet," Dora said. "Of course it had to be vague."

"Dora, you're full of it," Candace said. "You don't know what's going on here any more than we do. But if this *is* your God's plan, then your God sucks, and you suck for worshiping him."

"Girls," Penni said, looking around. "Can we—"

"How *dare* you," Dora said, glaring at Candace with fire in her eyes. "It's people like you who got us here. Wicked, lust-filled harlots who wipe their ass with the Bible."

"Crap," Jaclyn said, sniffing the air. She didn't smell any sleeping gas yet, but it had to be coming. "Ladies, we should really—"

Candace climbed over the table and slapped Dora in the face. Dora blinked a couple of times in shock. Then, in a surprising show of strength, she grabbed Candace by the arm and pulled her the rest of the way across the table. Candace bounced off the bench and hit the floor, landing on her back. She tried to sit up but Dora was already on top of her, slapping her repeatedly across the face.

Jaclyn stood up and started to run to their side of the table, but Penni was already there. The muscular woman grabbed Dora by the arm, pulled her off of Candace, and tossed her aside. Then she leaned down to help Candace up. "Are you okay?" Penni asked. Candace just stared past Penni, and her scratched-up face suddenly took on an expression of horror. Penni turned to see what she was looking at.

"Dora?" Jaclyn asked. One table over, Dora lay in a crumpled heap on the floor, her neck at an odd angle. She didn't appear to be breathing.

"Oh my god," Penni said, rushing over to Dora. "I'm sorry, I didn't mean it. She'll be okay. She'll be okay."

"Does anyone know CPR?" Candace asked, getting to her feet.

"I do," Jaclyn said. Penni moved out of her way as Jaclyn crouched over Dora. She knew right away it was a lost cause. Penni had thrown Dora hard, so hard she'd hit her neck on the next table. CPR wasn't going to fix this. But she had to try something. "Don't move her," Jaclyn said. "We need to keep her still until…"

The lights were getting dim. Except Jaclyn knew that wasn't the case, it was her eyelids that were getting heavy. *Not now*, she thought, as a familiar odor filled her nostrils. "We just… have… to…"

"God damn it!" Jaclyn screeched as she woke up. Getting out of bed, she called out, "Aisha, did Dora survive?"

"Unfortunately she did not," Aisha said. "She passed away from a neck injury."

"I could have saved her, you bitch," Jaclyn wailed. "If you hadn't gassed us, I could have saved her!"

"That is highly unlikely," Aisha replied. "I have observed that many humans blame themselves for events that were beyond their control. I assure you that Dora was beyond your ability to revive."

"I have to talk to Penni," Jaclyn said, sitting in front of the viewscreen.

"I'm afraid that's impossible," Aisha said. "She's currently undergoing a mental evaluation to determine if she's dangerous."

"What?" Jaclyn asked.

"She was directly responsible for Dora's death," Aisha said. "We need to be certain that it won't happen again."

"It was an accident," Jaclyn said. "She was protecting Candace."

"Intentional or not, we must keep such an event from happening again. If it was an accident, then she is capable of causing similar accidents in the future."

"Is there any way I can speak on her behalf?"

"The event was recorded from eight different camera angles. It is doubtful that you have any data that we do not."

Jaclyn thought for a moment. "If she's found guilty, how long until her sentence is carried out?"

"Your language indicates you think of this as a trial," Aisha said. "It is only an evaluation. It will most likely take several hours. If it is determined that her existence puts others in danger, she will be placed in stasis-sleep before her body is processed. She will go to bed as normal, and never wake up. The termination process is painless if that is your worry."

"My worry?" Jaclyn shouted incredulously. "Human beings are an endangered species, and you're talking about my friend like she's some sort of resource."

"Our goal is the survival of your species," Aisha said. "Humans who kill other humans do not further that goal."

"She's my friend, though," Jaclyn said.

"We understand," Aisha said. "You are afraid to lose a friend. Don't despair. There are thousands of humans on this ship. You will find other compatible friends."

Jaclyn tried to ignore Aisha's callous nature. She was a computer, after all, and incapable of understanding emotional attachments or even the sanctity of life. Jaclyn just felt so powerless, and hated that the Preservers had been so short-sighted. Leaving computers in charge of an operation like this, with no way for the rescued species to assume control... It would eventually lead to the deaths of every human they'd rescued.

"Aisha," Jaclyn asked. "What do you think will be the

outcome of Penni's mental assessment?"

"There is an eighty-nine percent probability that she will be terminated."

Jaclyn let out a long breath. "Aisha," she said. "If the Preservers on board were to wake up right now, would Penni be saved?"

"If the Preservers were to awaken, any of the computer's pending decisions would be voided," Aisha said. "They would study the logs, and they would determine Penni's fate. But as you have been informed, there is no way to awaken them in a non-emergency situation."

Jaclyn thought about that for a moment. Would the Preservers be as clinical as the computer? These aliens had invested a lot of their technology into saving other species, so they must have been capable of compassion. It was a gamble, but Jaclyn understood the odds. She knew what she had to do.

"Aisha, this situation is very upsetting," Jaclyn said. "I need to be somewhere calming. Is Meeting Room Seventeen available?"

"Meeting Room Seventeen is currently unoccupied," Aisha said. "If it will help calm your nerves, I will allow this change to your schedule."

The door to the hallway opened. Jaclyn tucked the viewscreen remote into her sleeve and stepped into the hallway.

Meeting Room Seventeen was the only common room in Jaclyn's section of the ship to have a window. Jaclyn entered and stood in front of the window, watching the stars. While she'd come with an ulterior motive, the view really was quite calming. The infinity of space had a way of putting her problems in perspective.

But that wasn't why she was here. Beside the window, there was an access panel on the wall. The metal plate was about a foot wide and three feet tall. She'd touched it before, and once she'd even tried to pry it open before being warned by the computer.

This isn't going to work, she told herself. But she had to try. It could mean saving Penni's life, as well as the lives of many future victims. The passengers couldn't go on with a computer acting as their judge and executioner. Someone with a heart had to be put in control.

Three... two... one... Jaclyn held her breath. As a swimmer, she'd spent a good deal of her youth underwater. At her peak, she'd been able to hold her breath for nearly five minutes. These days it was probably closer to four. But that was fine. She could accomplish a lot in four minutes.

She rushed for the metal plate, using a corner of the remote to pry it off the wall. It came off easier than she'd expected. A pair of vertical pipes lay behind it. Jaclyn didn't know if they were for water, power, or something else, but it didn't matter. With any luck, damaging the pipes would cause an emergency.

Aisha's voice spoke through invisible speakers. "Jaclyn, please return to your room."

Jaclyn dropped the remote and held the metal panel in two hands. She hacked at the pipes with it, hoping to cut through one of them. Each impact made a loud clang, and she wondered if any of the other passengers could hear it in their rooms.

The air looked fuzzy. Jaclyn refused to breathe, but she could see a haze in the air, and knew that it was filling with sleeping gas. She continued striking the pipes with her improvised tool. Unfortunately, she didn't seem to be making much of a dent.

Four large discs descended from the ceiling, each about the size of a tire. On the underside of each disc, a two-pronged claw snapped open. Jaclyn had seen these before, right before losing consciousness, but this was the first time she was able to make out any details. The claws were metal, but the inside of each prong was padded. Each claw was about the right size to close around a human waist. Jaclyn guessed that these floating claws allowed the ship to transport unconscious people back to their rooms.

One claw sped towards Jaclyn, its pincers open wide. She jumped to the side just before it hit the wall with a loud thud. It turned toward her but she rolled underneath it. As she got to her feet, she saw the other three rushing towards her.

Jaclyn paused for a moment. She knew she couldn't evade them forever, and she couldn't hold her breath much longer. She needed to end this, and fast.

I'm doing this for you, Penni, Jaclyn thought, standing in front of the window. The metal claws soared in her direction. At the last possible second, she dropped to the floor. Unable to hold her breath any longer, she took a deep breath of the gas-filled air.

The claws hit the window above her, shattering it to pieces. Air rushed out of the room, blowing the tables, the claws, and Jaclyn out into space. Drifting away from the ship, Jaclyn saw it from the outside for the first time. *It looks just like the flying saucers in the movies,* she thought. As darkness clouded the edges of her vision, she saw a metal panel slide closed over the window. Then the gas fully took effect, mercifully robbing her of her consciousness.

Penni woke up feeling stiff. She'd gotten used to grogginess when waking from stasis-sleep. It was a heavy feeling, like coming out of a coma. But this time was much worse. She felt like she'd been asleep for weeks. Strange half-dreams flitted from her mind, and it took her a few minutes to figure out what was real and what had just been a dream.

It all came back to her suddenly, like being hit with a bat. Dora. The psych evaluation. The computer hadn't been very forthcoming about the results, but when Penni had gone into stasis-sleep, she'd had the strange feeling that she'd never wake up.

Apparently she'd been worried for nothing. As she got out of bed, the viewscreen came on and her personal assistant appeared on the screen.

"Good morning," Pims said. "You've been in stasis-sleep for six years. We have landed on a planet, one which you will find is quite similar to Earth. I will fill you in on the details as you have your breakfast."

The viewscreen filled with images of a beautiful meadow, with a gentle stream flowing by a grove of oddly-colored trees. Two of the rescue ships were parked in the distance, and hundreds of humans flowed out of them, looking awed by their new surroundings. A pair of tall, thin, definitely-not-humans walked among them, looking just as impressed by this new world.

Penni ate her breakfast quickly, wanting nothing more than to feel actual wind on her face, and grass between her toes. Until just this moment, she hadn't realized how much she missed being outside. *Jaclyn was right*, she thought, remembering an earlier conversation about the importance of finding a planet. She couldn't wait to find Jaclyn and experience this new world with her.

Salvage

Violet was easily the least essential member of the salvage team. Derrick's mechanic skills had proven invaluable at keeping their equipment running, as well as fixing up whatever broken machines they recovered. Connor's intimidating physique and marine training kept the team safe from squatters and pirates. Both men were exceptionally strong, and while Violet was no weakling, she was like a four-year-old compared to the guys.

So what do I even bring to the party? Violet wondered, bringing the shuttle in for a landing. She was an excellent pilot, but Connor and Derrick could also fly the ship when needed. Maybe not as well, but it wasn't like they had to do a lot of fancy maneuvers. The truth was, she was here because her mother owned the company. Someday, hopefully far off in the future, Violet would take over Finch Salvage, and she needed to learn every aspect of the business.

It wasn't what she wanted, though. Owning a business didn't sound fun to her. Paperwork made her want to scream. All she'd ever wanted was to fly spaceships, and for the most part, she was happy with her current position. She just wished the guys would stop telling her how useless she was.

Connor wasn't so bad. If he saw Violet struggling to lift

something, he'd drop whatever he was doing and lend a hand. There was a condescending quality to his help, though, even though he never verbally criticized her. She always felt like he was silently judging her, but it could have been her imagination.

Derrick, though. He had a mouth that wouldn't quit. If he wasn't making fun of Violet's lack of strength, he was making nepotism jokes. She could have retaliated with jabs of her own, perhaps pointing out his gambling addiction. But that just wasn't in her. Not only did she not want to stoop to Derrick's level, but those kinds of insults just didn't come naturally to her.

She probably could have gotten Derrick fired with a single call, but she didn't want to run crying to mommy every time someone was mean to her. Besides, Derrick really was good at his job, and it would be hard to find someone to replace him.

The shuttle docked and the guys began unloading the tech they'd acquired. Violet grabbed a hoverdolly and started loading it up. But before she got far, her comm box dinged. "One sec, it's Mom," she said, answering the comm.

"Violet, I need you in my office right away," Ruby said.

Violet could see Derrick staring at her, the wheels turning in his head. He was going through his mental database of not-particularly-creative insults, picking the one best suited for the situation. "Mom, it won't take us long, I'll see you once the ship's unloaded."

"Let the boys do their job," Ruby said. "Yours is in here. We've got another contract, and it's a biggie."

"Sorry guys," Violet said, putting her comm back in her pocket.

"Slacker," Derrick muttered as she walked past.

"That's huge," Violet said, looking at the schematic. The ship had seven decks and was designed for a crew of ninety. "How much were the salvage rights?"

"That's the best part," Ruby said. "Not a single credit. They're even going to pay us."

Violet gave her a skeptical look. "What's the catch?"

"It's a science research vessel," Ruby said. "There was a problem with the engines, and the crew had to evacuate. Now the ship is in a decaying orbit over an uninhabited planet called Maeros. The ship is a lost cause, and the scientists have been reassigned to other stations. But they want their data. The ship's computers are full of research documents and such, and they didn't have time to copy it all before they evacuated. All we have to do is dock, download their data, and we can keep anything else we find."

"You're being conned, Mom." Ruby was pretty sharp for her age, but she wasn't impossible to fool. Sometimes Violet worried she'd have to take over the business sooner than expected.

"Look for yourself," Ruby said, and handed the paperwork over. She didn't mind being second-guessed by her daughter. It meant the girl was growing up to be a shrewd businesswoman.

Violet read over the contract. It was from a legitimate company, and the legalese appeared to be in order. Her expression gradually morphed from skeptical to awed. "Ten thousand credits?" Violet read out loud.

"If we get all the data," Ruby said. "But they've already sent over a five hundred credit advance. It's ours to keep even if the ship crashes before we get there."

"You keep saying 'we.' Are you coming with us on this one?"

"That's the plan," Ruby said. "It's a big ship. The more hands we've got, the more we can squirrel away before time runs out."

"And you're sure it's not dangerous?" Violet asked. "You said they had to evacuate..."

"They assure me that they were just acting in an abundance of caution," Ruby replied. "As long as we're in and out before the ship hits the planet's atmosphere, we'll be fine. It's going to be the easiest money we've ever made, I guarantee it."

From a distance, the research vessel Starweaver looked more like a space station than a ship. It was huge and brick-like, with some of the decks jutting out farther than others. The highest deck was the smallest, with floor-to-ceiling windows on all sides. Dozens of sensor arrays adorned the top of the ship.

"Kind of looks like a stack of books," Violet said.

"Now that you mention it, yeah," Derrick agreed.

Violet noted that Derrick refrained from calling her any colorful nicknames. It was amazing how much more civil he was when Ruby was in the room.

"There's the docking ports," Ruby said.

"On it," Violet replied. The vessel had eight ports, all of which were currently empty. As she approached the port, a light flashed on her control panel. "Their docking guide's offline," she said.

"Can you still connect?" Ruby asked.

"In my sleep," Violet said. "Switching to manual." She pulled up beside the larger ship, aligning its docking port with the Finch ship's starboard airlock. There was a bump, and the ship shuddered.

"Butterfingers," Derrick said. Ruby shot him a sharp look.

"Just making sure everyone's awake," Violet said. She made a few adjustments, then brought the ship as close to the science vessel as possible. "Engaging magnetic seal." There was another small shudder followed by a whooshing sound. "Locked."

"Perfect seal," Ruby said, glaring at Derrick. "Let's see you boys manage that."

"Yeah, well… she has her job, I have mine," Derrick said.

"Good job, Violet," Connor said, patting her on the shoulder.

"Check the air quality," Ruby said.

"I've done this before, Mom," Violet said, tapping a few more buttons. "Air's fine. Oxygen levels normal. Temperature's normal. No viral pathogens, no radiation. Gravity's fine. Everything looks good."

"Everyone make sure you're armed, just to be safe," Ruby said. Three of them carried standard shock pistols. Connor's holster held a Hyperbeam 311 Pocket Cannon, a powerful handgun of dubious legality. The four of them stood, checked the supplies in their packs and pouches, and approached the airlock.

Connor stood in front. Over the years, he had subconsciously assumed the role of the group's protector. He'd been ousted from the marines for failing to protect his team, and now he had a tendency to overcompensate, fearlessly taking point when danger was possible. While he didn't hope to die any time soon, when it was his time, he wanted to go out defending others.

The door whooshed open, and Connor was the first to enter the hall. Seeing that it was safe, he motioned for the others to join him. It was a nondescript hallway, with no signs of activity. The left wall was just one long window, from which they could see the nose of their ship and the infinity of space behind it. There were no other doors in the hall, other than the lift at the end of the hallway.

Their footsteps echoed on the metal floors, the only other sound being the hum of the ships environmental systems. All four salvagers were on edge. They'd spent years cannibalizing derelict spacecraft, but something about this one just felt wrong. It might have just been the size. The bigger a ship was, the stranger it felt to find it empty. It was like the difference between being the only customer in a restaurant, versus being the only person in an entire town.

They reached the end of the hallway and entered the lift. "Which floor?" Connor asked. A computer screen on the wall displayed a cross section of the ship, with their current level highlighted in red. They were docked on the lowest level, G. The ship's levels were listed beneath the map:

A: Observation Deck

B: Bridge / Command Offices

C: Offices

D: Specialized Labs / Airlock

E: General Labs / Project Rooms

F: Crew Quarters

G: Docking Bays

"Level D," Ruby said, and Connor tapped the screen. "We'll download their files, then proceed to level E to see if there are any other computers to access. I guess we'll hit the bridge too, in case they want the ship's logs. Then we can start looking for equipment to salvage."

They nodded in agreement, then stood in silence while the lift carried them up towards level D. After a minute, Connor said, "This lift sure is slow."

"Probably intentional," Derrick said. "They carry a lot of sensitive equipment back and forth. Can't have their explosive chemicals jostling when the lift suddenly stops."

"Any way to override it?" Ruby asked.

Derrick tapped a gear-shaped icon in the lower corner of the elevator's input screen. A settings menu popped up, but all the options were grayed out. Another pop-up asked them to insert a keycard to continue. "Not without clearance, it looks like," Derrick said.

Ruby frowned. "They assured me that all the command features would be unlocked," she said.

"Guess they forgot the lifts," Violet said.

They arrived on D deck and the doors slid open. Ruby consulted the map on her tablet and pointed in the direction of the records room. But when they reached the room, it wouldn't let them in without a keycard. Ruby cursed up a storm while Derrick started rooting through his bag for a cutting torch.

While they worked, Violet noticed a restroom on the

opposite side of the hallway. "I'll be right back," she told them, feeling the call of nature. As the restroom doors slid open, she noticed the lights were flickering. She looked up and saw several odd little divots in the walls and ceiling, like it had been damaged by corrosive chemicals.

Weird, Violet thought. Had someone's experiment gone wrong? But why in the bathroom? At least it hadn't melted all the way through the bulkhead. Turning away from the damage, she opened one of the stall doors and screamed.

A woman's body lay across the toilet. She was covered in horrific burns, with bits of bone showing through the holes in her jumpsuit. As Violet stared in horror, the restroom door opened and the rest of her crew rushed to her side.

"What happened here?" Ruby asked.

"Maybe they were working with acid," Connor said.

"In the bathroom?" Violet asked.

"Why didn't they move her body somewhere?" Derrick asked.

"Must have happened right around the time the engines failed," Ruby said. "They didn't have time to clean up all their messes."

"That can't be a coincidence," Violet said. "Whatever caused their engine troubles has to be related to this."

"She's got a keycard," Derrick said. Hooked to the woman's belt was a yellow card and an ID badge.

Ruby started to reach for the card. "Wait, Mom!" Violet said, and Ruby halted. Violet walked over to the sinks and pulled a pair of disposable rubber gloves out of a dispenser. She put them on and unhooked the keycard from the corpse's belt. She looked at the ID card. The dead woman's name was Doctor Krista Douglas, and her position was Director of Biological Studies.

"Let's go," Ruby said, and led them back to the records room. She swiped the keycard and the door opened.

"Stand back," Connor said, one hand on the holster on his belt. "Something's not..."

The records room wasn't very big, and consisted of a single computer and a dozen hard drives. But Connor's eyes were directed to the corpse in the corner, half hidden under the computer desk. This man was marred by burns similar to those on the woman in the bathroom. Connor moved farther into the room so the others could see.

"Maybe it's something in the air," Violet suggested. "One of their experiments might have released a corrosive cloud."

"Seems fine now," Derrick said, sniffing the air.

Ruby retrieved a second keycard from the corpse and handed it to Connor. "In case we get separated," she said. Then she retrieved two memory sticks from her pocket and stuck them into the computer, quickly downloading the entire hard drive onto the sticks. When the transfers were done, she handed the second stick to Violet. "And that's in case one gets corrupted," she said. Ruby didn't mess around when it came to backups.

"Huh," Violet said, looking at the computer screen. "It looks like he was in the middle of typing a log when he died." She scrolled up through the log and started reading. "He says they found something on the planet below and brought it on board the ship, but it got loose."

"Something?" Connor asked, poking his head back out in to the hall.

"A life form," Violet said. "He says they didn't know it was alive until it was too late. They kept it quarantined, but it escaped."

"Does he say what it looked like?" Derrick asked.

"All he says is—" Violet began, but Ruby screamed. They all turned toward her and followed her line of sight.

There was an air vent above the dead scientist, and a clear ooze now poured from the grate, slowly flowing down the wall. As the four salvagers stepped backward, the slime enveloped the corpse. The jelly-like substance undulated like a living organism.

"Get behind me," Connor whispered, drawing his gun. As

the rest of the team fled into the hall, he fired several shots at the creature, but they didn't seem to have any effect.

"Get to the lift," Ruby said, and the four of them headed down the hall. When the doors didn't automatically open, Ruby kept hitting the button. "Come on, come on," she muttered. It took a good thirty seconds for the lift to arrive, which struck Ruby as odd, since it should have already been on their floor.

They filed into the lift and Ruby pressed the button for the bridge. As the doors began to close they saw something lurch out of the records room. The corpse of the scientist now shuffled toward the lift, completely enveloped by the slime. It moved as if the ooze itself was controlling the body. The slime on one leg would undulate, pulling that foot forward. The jelly on the arms would shift to regain the corpse's balance, then the other leg would shift forward. It wasn't very quick, but it was probably faster than the ooze could have moved on its own.

The doors took their own sweet time closing, and the creature was less than a meter away when the lift finally started moving. No one spoke for several seconds. It was Violet who broke the silence. "Why the bridge?" she asked. "We need to get out of here."

"To look at the ship's logs," Ruby said. "We've been lied to. I want to know the rest of the story."

"The rest of the story is we head back to our ship and go home," Violet said.

"What about the salvage?" Derrick asked.

"W-What?" Violet sputtered. "Are you serious right now?"

"We got this far," Connor said.

"Dot," Ruby said. "Sorry, I mean Violet. You have to understand. Business has been in the red for a while. I've only kept us afloat this long with some creative bookkeeping. This is our chance to finally get back in the black. Finch Salvage is my legacy to you. I can't leave you a failing business."

"Mom, you know I don't care how successful you are," Violet said. "I just want you to be happy and safe. And I don't think that's going to happen if we stay here."

"I appreciate that," Ruby said. "But there's a degree of danger in all our jobs. Sometimes Connor's fending off space pirates, while Derrick's removing valuable equipment from a structure that could collapse any minute, and then you're flying the shuttle around asteroids."

"Ugh," Violet said. "This plot doesn't make any sense. Why would Ruby risk her daughter's life when there's monsters crawling around?"

"Was that in character?" Brant asked.

"No, sorry," Dot said. The rest of the gaming group stared at her in confusion. Dot was used to being stared at, but usually it was for other reasons. "It's just, it's one thing to watch people make dumb decisions in a horror movie. But when you're actually playing the characters, the stupidity is that much more obvious."

"I get you," Rita said. "But if we went back to our ship right now, the adventure would be over. We've only been playing for half an hour." Rita and Dot had been dating for over a year, but this was the first time Rita had seen her get so upset over a role-playing game.

"And I spent thirty bucks on this module," Brant added. They were taking a break from their weekly Blaggards & Blades game to try a sci-fi themed one-shot.

"I guess it's just me," Dot said. "Our B&B characters are pretty one-dimensional. But these feel more like real people, and it's easier to see the flaws in their motivations."

"I think you're doing fine," Robert said. "Violet's the only one who isn't motivated by money. She *should* object. Derrick, for one, has a huge gambling debt. The slime zombies aren't much scarier to him than the goons his loan shark sends after him."

"Please don't call them slime zombies," Brant said.

"What are they really called?" Sharon asked.

"Well, the book calls them plasmonic puppets, but your characters wouldn't know that," Brant said.

"Then until we have a name, they're slime zombies," Sharon said. "And Dot, I think Ruby's pretty consistent. Her business problems are bigger than she's ever told Violet, because she didn't want her to worry. But deep down, she believes it's worth the danger to keep from leaving her daughter in debt."

"And Connor wants to die," Rita added. "Maybe not right away, but he still feels guilty for the acts that got him booted out of the marines. Now he wants to go out fighting, protecting someone else. He wants to be remembered as a hero."

"So yeah," Brant said. "It makes sense for Violet to object, but she's going to get voted down."

"Fair enough," Dot said. "Let's get back to it, then."

The lift reached the bridge and the doors opened. Right away they spotted a problem. The ship's navigation console was smashed, as was communications.

"This doesn't look like acid burns," Derrick said, examining the wreckage. "In fact, I'd say someone used a crowbar."

"Who would do that, though?" Connor wondered aloud.

Ruby moved to the command console. "Damn," she said. "Someone's deleted all the ship's logs."

"Environmental still works," Violet said, studying another computer screen. "At least we don't have to worry about losing life support. This is weird, though. Someone intentionally raised the temperature by fifteen degrees. I thought it felt warm in here."

"Uh oh," Ruby said, studying the command screen. "I just did a scan for life signs, and it looks there's three other humans still alive on the ship."

"Where?" Connor asked.

"Here's one on the crew level, in one of the cabins," Ruby pointed to a red dot on the screen. "And here's one in the medlab on Level E, but their heartbeat is really slow. They might be in a coma. And this one's on the office level, moving down a hallway."

"Can that computer tell you where all the slime creatures are?" Violet asked.

"No," Ruby said. "It just tracks these implants the scientists have. As long as they have a heartbeat, it transmits their location to the bridge."

"We should get down there right away," Connor said. "Maybe we can save a few lives."

"Bet there's a reward for that, too," Derrick added.

"We should go after the one on the crew level first," Violet said. "The one that's moving might not be there by the time we get there, and the one in the lab might not be savable."

"Sounds like a plan," Ruby said. "But first I want to check out the captain's office. See if they have a personal computer."

The office was located just behind the bridge. They found the captain sitting in her chair, dead. "She's been shot in the head," Connor said.

"Suicide?" Derrick asked.

"Maybe," Connor said. "But I don't see a gun anywhere, do you?"

"So probably not suicide," Violet said.

"Let me check her personal logs," Ruby said. But it was no use. Her computer had also been wiped. She reached down and took the captain's keycard, then handed it to Violet. "The captain's keycard will open any door on this ship," she said. "Violet, if the rest of us don't make it, I want you to do whatever you can to stay alive. Promise me."

"I'm not leaving without you, Mom," Violet answered.

Ruby stared hard into her eyes. "Promise me," she

repeated.

Violet nodded. "I promise."

Thanks to the captain's keycard, a much quicker lift ride took them to the crew level. From the lift, the main hallway extended in both directions, then split into two halls, each of which split again. It would have taken forever to search every room, but they knew which one they needed to find. The doors closest to the elevator led to the break room, some restrooms, laundry, and something called a "hologram lounge."

"Keep your eyes open," Connor said. He walked with his weapon drawn, ready to fire at any movement. Of course, his gun hadn't hurt the creature before, but it still helped him feel in control.

"We've only seen one creature so far," Derrick said. "Maybe it can't use the lifts. If we just don't go back to that floor…"

"Yeah, like they'd print a module with just one monster in it," Ruby said.

"Stay in character," said a voice from above, and they went back to exploring the hallway.

Derrick poked his head into the break room on their way by. The room held four tables, each surrounded by chairs. On the back wall were three vending machines, a sink, a fridge, and some cabinets. Some of the chairs were overturned, and the vending machines had been smashed. "One minute," he said. Before the others could stop him, he walked up to the vending machine, reached past the broken glass, and grabbed a handful of chocolate bars.

"Don't go wandering off," Connor admonished him, as he returned to the hallway.

"Might need the quick energy later," Derrick said unapologetically. "Now who wants a candy bar?"

Each of them took one, and they continued walking. They passed more than a dozen doors, and Derrick kept wanting to enter each one to see if any valuables were easily grabbable. "Let's find the survivor first, and then we'll talk," Connor said.

When they finally reached the right room, Ruby swiped her card. The door wouldn't open. Then Violet swiped the captain's keycard. The light above the slot flashed green, but the door still wouldn't open. "Weird," Violet said.

"Let me try something," Connor said. He knocked on the door.

"Go away," cried a muffled voice from the other side of the door.

"I guess he doesn't want our help," Derrick said. "Can I go loot some rooms now?"

"He's going to get rescued whether he likes it or not," Connor said. "Derrick, do your thing."

Derrick huffed and went through his gear bag. He retrieved a cutting torch and began working at the door's edges.

"I said go away!" the voice repeated as Derrick drew a rectangular line of superheated metal around the door. When it was complete, the salvage team moved out of the way as the large slab of metal fell outward, clanging on the hallway floor. They peeked through the door.

A haggard-looking man stared back at them, his eyes full of desperation and fear. He wore the same jumpsuit as the other scientists, but his was soiled and soaked with sweat. He looked like he hadn't shaved for several days, and his skin was sallow. Connor stepped through the doorway. The room reeked. There was a bucket in one corner, which the scientist had been using as a toilet. The floor was covered with empty candy bar wrappers and potato chip bags. The room's only air vent had a sheet of metal welded over it.

"Who... who are you people?" the survivor asked.

"Connor Pine," the ex-marine said, holding his hand out. The scared scientist didn't take it.

Ruby entered behind Connor. "I'm Ruby Finch," she said.

"We've been sent to rescue you." It wasn't a complete lie. Part of being in the salvage business was looking for survivors and getting them to safety. That responsibility was written into most salvage contracts. "And you are?"

"Doomed, now," the man said. "I'm... I'm Doctor Nathan Karat. I... why did you do that... I was safe... safe..."

"Your ship is going to crash into the planet below," Violet said, stepping through the door. "Believe me, you'll be safer with us."

"But those... *things* are out there," he said. "We'll never make it out of here."

"You have a better chance with us than alone," Connor said.

While the rest of the team gave the doctor a pep talk, Derrick looked up and down the hallway. Personal crew quarters lay behind every door. *Surely some of them are unlocked,* Derrick thought. He tried three doors before one opened. No one was inside, and there were no signs of monsters. The room had two sets of bunk beds and two cluttered desks. Derrick heard cash register noises in his head as he appraised every item he saw.

A pair of Heliosands sunglasses, fifty credits. A classic Swiss watch, two hundred credits. A pair of night vision goggles, five hundred credits. A laptop gaming computer, eight hundred credits at least. He started stuffing items into his bag, oblivious to the slime oozing out of the air vent behind him.

Ruby was a smooth talker, and she was starting to make headway with Doctor Karat when they heard a scream. Connor was the first one back in the hallway. One of the doors was open a few rooms down. As Connor watched, another one of those slime zombies stepped out of the room. Only this time, Connor recognized the corpse right away.

"And that's why you don't split the party," Brant said.

"I know, I know" Robert said. "But I had to stay true to

his character. I guess I'll take over Doctor Karat now."

"That'll work," Brant said.

Connor fired at the monster while the other three ran for their lives. His shots made bloody holes appear in Derrick's acid-burned flesh, but he didn't seem to be hurting the creature itself. When he was sure his teammates were at a safe distance, he turned and ran after them.

"Where to?" Violet asked as Connor burst into the lift.

"Level E," Ruby said. As the doors slid shut, they got one last look at Derrick lurching down the hall.

"God speed, old friend," Connor said, and the lift began to move.

Floor E contained various labs and project rooms. As the doors opened, right away they saw a corpse in the hallway. One entire leg was gone, but there wasn't any slime on it at the moment. Several acid burns adorned the walls and floor, but none of the monsters were in sight.

"Which way?" Connor asked, and Ruby pointed down the hall. As quietly as they could, they walked through the hallways until they found the medlab. As they were about to enter, they heard a scratching sound behind them, from the door on the opposite side of the hallway.

"Wait," Connor said, turning around. The door was labeled "Animal Studies."

"Don't open it!" Karat shouted. "It could be one of those monsters!"

"Right," Connor said. "And if it is, I'd rather face it head on than have it sneak up behind us while we're in the medlab."

The others looked worried, but they agreed. Connor readied his useless weapon, and reached forward to press the button.

The doors opened and a green glow erupted from the darkness. Something furry leaped through the doorway, ran between Connor's legs and vanished down the hallway.

"Thanks for the heart attack," Violet said. "What was that thing?"

"Looked like a ferret," Ruby said.

"His name is Rudy," Doctor Karat said. "Short for Rudolph. Well, 'Subject RDF four one one three.' We try not to name the lab animals, but he was very popular with the scientists. He has bioluminescent fur."

"Why are you making glow-in-the-dark ferrets?" Violet asked.

"Ah, well," Karat said. "There's caves on the planet below, and we were going to train the ferrets to—"

"Later," Ruby interrupted. "Let's check out the medlab."

"Wait," Violet said, nodding toward the animal studies lab. "The bridge computer didn't tell us about the ferret. What if there's more animals still alive in there?"

"So?" Connor asked.

"We can't just let them all die," Violet said.

"Oh," Ruby said. She put her hand on Violet's shoulder. "Tell you what. Humans first, then animals. Okay?"

Violet reluctantly agreed, and they entered the medlab. There were four metal tables in the center of the room, two of which had bodies on them. Both bodies were covered in burns.

"Guess we're too late," Connor said.

Doctor Karat studied the corpses. "These look like they've been dead for a while. I doubt either one is the person you detected from the bridge."

"Then where did..." Violet began, then noticed something. "What are those?" she asked, pointing at four round protrusions on the wall.

"Stasis tubes," Karat answered. "If someone's injured and we don't have the means to save them, it slows down their biological processes until proper care arrives."

"One's blinking," Violet said, indicating a flashing light.

"Hmm..." Karat said. He studied a nearby computer

screen. "Doctor Kyla Skye. I know her. I didn't know she was injured. It doesn't say what her injuries are…"

"Open it," Ruby said.

"If she's injured, she's better off in stasis," Karat said.

"Not when this ship hits the planet's atmosphere," Connor said.

"Fair point," Karat replied, tapping a few keys on the computer. The tube slid out from the wall, and the hatch opened. The woman inside had black hair and wore a blue jumpsuit. After a few seconds, her eyes started to flutter. Then she sat up suddenly, gasping for air.

"Are th-they gone?" she asked.

"The gelatinous creatures?" Karat asked, and she nodded. "I'm afraid not. Is that why you were in stasis?"

"Th-they don't like cold," Kyla said, shivering. "I thought if I lowered muh-my body temperature, they wuh-wouldn't find me."

"Good plan," Connor said.

"Th-then put me back in until help arrives," Kyla said, her voice tinged with panic. "There's three more tuh-tubes, suh-some of you can join me."

"I'm afraid we are the help," Violet said. "This ship is going to burn up. You'd better come with us."

Kyla nodded, and they helped her out of the tube. Her legs were a bit shaky at first, and she leaned on Violet for support.

"Are there any weapons on board this ship?" Connor asked.

"There's an armory," Karat said. "But it's probably picked clean by now. And none of our weapons seemed to hurt the creatures anyway."

"Wuh-we could try cold," Kyla suggested. She was starting to warm up, but her teeth were still chattering. "Su-some of the fuh-fire extinguishers use freezing foam."

"Good idea," Ruby said. "We'll head for the bridge and grab any extinguishers we find on the way."

Connor looked around the medlab and spotted an extinguisher. He removed it from the wall and held it like a weapon.

"Why the bridge?" Kyla asked. "Don't you huh-have a ship?"

"We detected one more human life on board," Ruby said. "But that was a while ago, and they were moving. We need to use the bridge's scanner to see where they are now."

Kyla nodded weakly and followed them out the door. As they entered the hallway, they heard more scratching from the animal studies lab.

"How many ferrets do you have?" Violet asked.

"That sounds… bigger," Karat answered.

"Everybody stand back," Connor said. He readied his fire extinguisher and pressed the button to open the door. Before it was completely open, a dark shape burst forward and grabbed Connor's face. He fired the extinguisher blindly, covering Doctor Karat with cold foam.

Connor fell to the floor, and the slime-covered chimpanzee sat on his chest, tearing into his face with its powerful acidic hands.

Violet spotted another extinguisher farther down the hall, and ran to retrieve it. She returned and sprayed the chimp with a powerful blast of foam. It turned its attention on her, but it was already starting to slow down. Violet kept spraying until the chimp was unrecognizable, just a foamy white blob with arms. It attempted one last leap towards Violet, but it fell flat on its face and lay still.

It was too late to save Connor. The creature had ripped his face to shreds, and his body shuddered as he took his final ragged breaths.

"I guess he died the way he wanted," Rita said.

"Getting mauled by a jelly-covered chimp?" Robert asked.

Rita playfully punched his arm. "Protecting the team, I mean."

"You want to take over Kyla?" Brant offered, and Rita nodded. He handed her a character sheet.

"What's that foam doing to me?" Robert asked.

"Looks like he mostly got your leg," Brant said. "But you can't wipe it off. It's an adhesive foam that sticks to the fabric. It'll evaporate in about an hour. Until then, you'll be walking with a limp. That's half-speed. Oh, and Violet? In your panic, you drained the fire extinguisher."

"Are there any more in the hallway?" Dot asked.

"You remember seeing one on the wall near the lift," Brant said. "But you might want to hurry. You hear a shuffling sound from down the other hallway..."

Beyond the medlab, some of the hallway lights had gone out. As the four survivors watched, a glow appeared in the distance. Rudy the ferret came running towards them. When it saw Kyla, it jumped into her arms and climbed onto her shoulder.

But farther down the hallway, a pair of humanoid shapes lurched towards them. "Let's go," Ruby said, and they ran for the lift. Violet was the first to reach the fire extinguisher. Ruby pressed the lift button, and Kyla ran aboard. Doctor Karat limped after them, dragging his frozen leg. The creatures were getting closer.

Violet ran back to help Karat. She put his arm over her shoulder and together they hobbled a little faster. As they reached the end of the hall, Violet shoved him into the lift, then turned around. The creatures were almost upon her. She gave two quick blasts with the extinguisher, and they backed off a bit.

"Violet, hurry!" Ruby shouted. Violet backed into the lift, keeping the extinguisher aimed at the goo-encrusted corpses. They started towards her again, but the lift doors closed.

They reached the bridge a few seconds later, and Rub

headed straight for the command console. "Scanning…" she said. "Huh. I can't find that third survivor. No more human life signs are detected."

"One of those things must have got them," Violet said.

"Let's get back to our ship, then," Ruby said. As soon as the words were out of her mouth, the ship shook, alarm klaxons started wailing, and red lights flashed all over the bridge.

"Someone has a flair for the dramatic," Violet said.

Ruby studied the readout on the command console. "There's been explosive decompressions on decks G and F," she said.

"Then we can't get to our ship," Violet said.

"Not good, not good, not good," Karat said, holding the sides of his head. Kyla patted him on the shoulder, trying to calm him down.

"There's an airlock on deck D," Ruby said. "If we put on some pressure suits…"

"There's only two suits in that airlock," Kyla said. "There's more in storage, but that's halfway across the ship."

"What about escape pods?" Violet asked.

"Also D deck," Ruby said. "We should head there immediately."

"Those pods are practically space coffins," Kyla said. "They hold about three days of air. You don't want to get into one unless you know help is coming."

"So we send out a distress signal," Violet offered.

"The communications console was destroyed," Ruby said. "And a lot of other systems are down. This looks intentional."

"Sabotage?" Violet asked. She turned to the doctors. "Have any of the other scientists been behaving suspiciously?"

The ship shook again.

"We'll play detective later," Ruby said. "We just lost E

deck. Right now we need to get out of here before we lose D deck. I propose you three get into escape pods. I'll put on a pressure suit and spacewalk out to our ship. Once I take off, I'll pick you up."

"I'll do the spacewalk," Violet said. "You three escape."

"Violet—" Ruby started.

"No arguments," Violet said. "I'm the pilot; flying is my thing. And I've logged way more spacewalk time than you have."

Ruby relented, proud to see her daughter taking charge of the situation.

"You arrive on D deck," Brant said. "As you step off the lift…"

"Is D deck where we saw that first slime zombie?" Robert asked.

"Right," Dot said. "I found the corpse in the bathroom, then we got the data, and the slime came out of the vent."

"We never killed that one," Sharon said.

"Is it still in the area?" Robert asked.

"You don't see it," Brant said. "In fact, the hallway is eerily quiet. You reach the escape pod bay and find…"

The pods were gone. Kyla checked the inventory monitor, and found that they'd all been launched empty.

"Why would anyone do that?" Violet asked. "They could have saved more lives if… oh. Probably the same person who sabotaged the engines and communications."

"Do you keep any spare pods anywhere?" Ruby asked.

"Hold on," Karat said. There were multiple storage closets in the room. One of them required special access, but Violet's keycard opened it. The hatch slid open, revealing two escape pods. The cylindrical metal tubes were a little over two meters long and surprisingly lightweight for their size. Working together, the four survivors pulled each cylinder across the room, sticking the ends into round recesses on the wall. Then they opened the hatches on the pods.

"You two," Ruby said, pointing to the scientists.

"No," Violet said. "You and Karat. He can barely walk, much less spacewalk. And you're... you know... older."

"Our ship has a biometric lock," Ruby said. "Only we can start it. If one of us doesn't make it, the other will."

"Well, that's contrived," Violet said.

"Shush," came a godlike voice from above.

With no further arguments, the two doctors got into their pods. Kyla held the ferret close to her chest as the pod closed. Then Ruby tapped a few buttons on the console, and the pods were pulled into the wall and launched into space.

"It's up to us now," Violet said.

They walked back into the hallway, only to find that they were surrounded. To their left, two slimy corpses shuffled forward. A third stood on their right, blocking their way to airlock.

"Let's do this," Ruby said. Both armed with fire extinguishers, they ran toward the solitary creature, blasting it with foam. It took a slow swipe at them as they ran by, just grazing Ruby's shoulder. The fabric on her jumpsuit sizzled.

They reached the airlock and closed the door behind them. Two pressure suits hung in one recessed corner, behind a clear sealed door. They retrieved the suits and hurriedly helped each other put them on. By the time they got to the helmets, they heard banging and scratching on the door. They skipped the standard safety checklist, and punched the airlock button as soon as the suits were sealed. Once all the air was sucked out of the room, the ship's outer doors opened, and the two slowly walked toward the exit hatch.

Each kept their fire extinguisher clipped to their pressure suit's belt, and they had a meter-long lead clipped between them to keep from getting separated. Their boots had magnetic soles, which they used to walk along the side of the research vessel. As they walked away from the exit hatch, the ship shuddered again. "I think we just lost pressure in D deck," Violet said into the suit's communicator.

Slowly and carefully, they walked toward the Finch Salvage ship. Each step seemed infuriatingly slow, and the science vessel looked dangerously close to the planet's atmosphere. They were halfway to the ship when Ruby heard a beeping sound from inside her suit. A digital readout in her helmet informed her that she was losing air pressure.

"What is it, Mom?" Violet asked.

"I've got a hole somewhere," she said. Then she saw it. Her shoulder, where she'd been hit by a creature earlier. Some of the goo must have gotten on her clothes, and now it had eaten through her pressure suit.

"We're halfway there," Violet said. "Do you think we can make it in time?"

"I don't think so," Ruby said. "I'm already down to forty percent."

"Is there a patching kit?" Violet asked. "Some sort of self-sealing whatzit?"

"Not that I know of," Ruby said. "Look, Violet, if I don't make it…"

"No!" Violet said. "Don't talk like that. We'll get you out of this." She put her hand on Ruby's shoulder, holding the hole shut, but air continued to escape through the rupture.

"…I want you to know how proud I am of you," Ruby finished.

And then Violet shot her.

"You do what?" Brant asked.

"The freezing foam," Dot said. "From my fire extinguisher. I blast it over the rupture in her suit. It seems pretty sticky, it should make a good seal. At least temporarily."

"Would that work?" Sharon asked.

"I... I..." Brant said, flipping back and forth through the rulebook. "I... guess? But you'll take four points of cold damage, and you won't be able to use that arm for a couple of hours."

"Good thinking," Rita said, patting Dot on the shoulder.

They reached the ship with no further incidents. The starboard airlock was still attached to the research vessel, so they walked across the hull and entered through the portside airlock. Once aboard, they removed their pressure suits and strapped themselves in. After they disengaged from the larger ship, they began scanning for the escape pods.

"There they are," Violet said after about twenty minutes. The research vessel was now entering the planet's atmosphere, but the escape pods were still at a safe distance. "Mom, get the airlock ready. We'll have to use the magnetic cables to latch onto the pods and pull them to us."

Ruby unlatched her harness and stood up. There was an odd popping sound, and she screamed. Blood spattered across the ship's viewscreen, and Violet turned to see her mother with a gaping hole in her chest. "Mom!" she shouted, as Ruby fell to the floor.

"Move and you're dead," came a man's voice. He stepped over Ruby's body and moved to stand next to the pilot's station. He was in his mid-fifties, with white hair and a beard. In one hand he held a metal cannister, and in the other he held a powerful-looking handgun. The latter was pointed at Violet's head.

"You killed my mother," Violet said, tears blurring her vision.

"I'll do worse than that," the man said. "I've been behind everything. It was I, Doctor Willick Saffron, who disabled the engines. I'm the one who brought the creatures aboard the ship. It was my genius that—"

* * *

"Max thrusters, straight ahead, go," Dot said.

"But he's in the middle of his speech," Brant objected.

"Then he's less likely to notice me hitting the button," Dot replied.

Brant sighed. "Fine. Your shuttle shoots forward at top speed. Doctor Saffron, the mastermind who was planning to sell these creatures to the military, is thrown against the back wall of your ship and takes… thirty-three damage. And you need to make a con save against the G forces."

"Twenty-one," Dot replied.

"Good enough," Brant said. "Saffron is stunned, but he isn't finished yet. He raises his weapon and…"

"Full stop, then reverse thrusters," Dot said. "Max speed, this time backwards."

Brant scowled. "He's thrown against the back of your pilot's seat, for… twenty-six damage. That finishes him off. With his last gasp, he starts telling you how he managed to breed the creatures in secret while—"

"Full speed forward again," Dot said. "Just to be sure."

"Hmmm," Brant said, rolling some dice. "You have turned Doctor Saffron into chunky salsa. You'll be cleaning bits of him out of your ship for weeks."

"Nice," Rita said, giving her girlfriend a high five. "Now come pick us up."

"Okay," Brant said. "So you go and pick up the two escape pods. Violet, Kyla, and Karat watch the research vessel burn up in the planet's atmosphere, happy to be alive, but sad for everyone they lost along the way."

"What about that cannister the bad guy was holding?" Dot asked.

"Well, if you'd given him a chance to explain," Brant said, "He would have told you that it was a sample of the slime creatures. He was going to find somewhere else to breed them, now that the ship was overrun."

"That's going right out the airlock," Dot said.

"Question," Rita said. "How was he planning to get off the science ship before we arrived?"

"That's why you were hired," Brant said. "He needed someone to bring him a ship, but it had to be a small group, people who wouldn't be noticed if they went missing. Saffron had this other company he was working for, and they forged the salvage offer. He was going to explain all of this until you just—"

"Good game," Robert said. "I loved the tension. You should run it again next week, but this time let us play as a bunch of soldiers who were sent to wipe out the monsters."

"Oooh, that sounds fun," Sharon said.

"I'll think about it," Brant said. "Well, that wraps it up for today. Ready to go?"

Robert and Sharon packed up their things, and the three left in Brant's car, leaving Dot and Rita alone.

"You saved me," Rita said, pulling Dot over to the couch.

"Yeah," Dot said, sounding forlorn. "I couldn't save my mother though."

"Don't make this weird," Rita said, pulling Dot in for a kiss.

And then they started a different sort of roleplaying.

Author's Notes

Spoilers abound, so read the stories first.

Escapism

I've never been to an escape room, nor have I watched any of the horror movies about them. So if I've ripped any of them off here, it's unintentional. I didn't plan this story ahead of time. The first puzzle, with the glow-in-the-dark paint, came to me in a dream, and I just started typing the story as I thought of it. Finding the ending was hard. It almost stopped right when they discovered the mall was also a giant escape room. That might have worked in a movie, but it didn't feel right in the story. So I kept going just a little longer.

All four characters are named after my cats.

Survivors

Some readers are going to be mad that I never explicitly explain what caused the apocalypse. But the story isn't about the disaster, it's about the antagonist's ego and entitlement. The apocalypse is just the setting.

Third Shift

I've always loved the idea that there's another side to the world, with unknown things walking around behind every wall, taking our place every time we leave a room. The thought of stumbling onto these things by accident is terrifying. "Sorry, human, wrong place, wrong time, you weren't supposed to see this." I realize that making the main character non-binary doesn't really add anything to the story, but that's kind of the point. Too many authors think there has to be an in-story reason for the main character not to be a cis, binary, straight, white male.

Forever Home

I have a lot of if/then beliefs. For example, I don't believe in God. But if there *is* a supreme being, I believe they're accepting of LGBTQIA+ people. This short story is based on another of my if/then beliefs: I don't believe in ghosts, but if ghosts *do* exist, I believe that cats can see them.

Dixieland

I don't know what I dreamed, but one morning I woke up with two words on my lips: Zombie fairies. Naturally I had to write it down.

Telethon

Some of the best superhero stories are the ones where the hero is the one who needs saving. I'll admit the bad guy's fate is a little dark. I kept it because the villain knew the secret to taking away the hero's powers, and I wanted to tie up the loose ends.

Social Cues

To some extent, the main character of this story is an author avatar. Does that make it self-serving that she ends up saving the world? Do I care?

Ray's Personal Blog

I was originally going to post this to a creepypasta website, but chickened out. The part with the closet light is based on true events.

Traveler

I can think of a few sci-fi shows that inspired this one, but for the most part I just wanted to do a multiverse story. I'll admit it's a little exposition-heavy, but this is the kind of short story that begs to become a series in itself.

Justice

More wish fulfillment. I like stories where bad things happen to bad people. I had a hard time justifying the ending to myself. After all, if the rich people had to be bullied into being better people, that's just another version of "might equals right." If it was wrong for one side, then it should wrong for the other. We can rationalize it by saying it's different when it's the marginalized group doing the bullying, but it still doesn't send a great message.

But the bottom line is, I truly don't think the world needs billionaires in it, when so many people are suffering in poverty. So I'm not going to lose sleep feeling sorry for the super wealthy.

Mutiny

This story is meant to be a little cheesy, with the hero and villain quipping at each other like comic book characters. I'm a lot of things, but subtle isn't one of them. When people examine my work 100 years from now (ha ha), I don't think there's going to be much debate over who the Crimson Caps represent.

The Preservers

This started with the concept that one person's heaven is another person's hell. I hate to say it, but as a loner, the situation presented in this story actually appeals to me. Free room and board, with unlimited movies? Of course, I'm probably fooling myself. It sounds good in a daydream, but it would suck in real life.

Salvage

When editing this story, I came across a few minor plot holes that I didn't bother to fix. The reason? It's an RPG module; it's not going to be airtight. So don't ask me why the chimp zombie was so much faster than the human zombies, when they were being manipulated by the same slime creatures. The answer is going to be, "Because that's what it said in the monster's stat block."

The sci-fi part of this story is based on an RPG module I wrote, which in turn was inspired by an old computer game. The modern part of the story is a sequel to a story from Geek Cutes, but it's okay if you haven't read that one first.

Special thanks to Kaius.

About the Author

Xine Fury is… standing right behind you!

Made ya look.

Also By Xine Fury

The following books by Xine Fury are also available:
    Bloodhunters v1: Bad Blood
    Bloodhunters v2: Blue Blood
    Bloodhunters v3: New Blood
    Blood Samples (A Bloodhunters Prequel)
    Geek Cutes
    Gender Rolls
    Side Quests
    Nomads of Zyden

Find them here: bit.ly/XineFury